W9-BVM-504

"GET OUT OF MY TOWN, SOLDIER!"

The man in the pearl-gray suit walked with a rolling strut to Matt Kincaid's table and stood there silently.

"Something you want?" asked Lt. Kincaid.

"I'm Frank Toomey," the tall man said, "and I want you out of my town."

Matt slowly smiled. "Sorry, it's not your town. And I'm not one of your hired morons."

Toomey reached across the table and grabbed Kincaid's neckerchief. "Look here, soldier..."

But Toomey wasn't used to the like of Lt. Matt Kincaid. The neckerchief was as far as he got...

EASY COMPANY

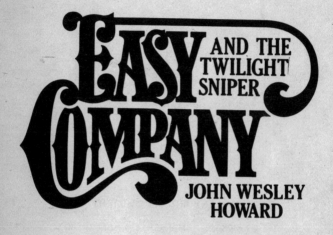

EASY COMPANY
AND THE TWILIGHT SNIPER

JOHN WESLEY HOWARD

A JOVE BOOK

EASY COMPANY AND THE TWILIGHT SNIPER

A Jove Book / published by arrangement with
the author

PRINTING HISTORY
Jove edition / September 1982

All rights reserved.
Copyright © 1982 by Jove Publications, Inc.
This book may not be reproduced in whole or in part,
by mimeograph or any other means, without permission.
For information address: Jove Publications, Inc.,
200 Madison Avenue, New York, N. Y. 10016.

ISBN: 0-515-06352-5

Jove books are published by Jove Publications, Inc.,
200 Madison Avenue, New York, N. Y. 10016. The words
"A JOVE BOOK" and the "J" with sunburst are trademarks
belonging to Jove Publications, Inc.

PRINTED IN THE UNITED STATES OF AMERICA

*Also in the EASY COMPANY series
from Jove*

EASY COMPANY AND THE SUICIDE BOYS
EASY COMPANY AND THE MEDICINE GUN
EASY COMPANY AND THE GREEN ARROWS
EASY COMPANY AND THE WHITE MAN'S PATH
EASY COMPANY AND THE LONGHORNS
EASY COMPANY AND THE BIG MEDICINE
EASY COMPANY IN THE BLACK HILLS
EASY COMPANY ON THE BITTER TRAIL
EASY COMPANY IN COLTER'S HELL
EASY COMPANY AND THE HEADLINE HUNTER
EASY COMPANY AND THE ENGINEERS
EASY COMPANY AND THE BLOODY FLAG
EASY COMPANY ON THE OKLAHOMA TRAIL
EASY COMPANY AND THE CHEROKEE BEAUTY
EASY COMPANY AND THE BIG BLIZZARD
EASY COMPANY AND THE LONG MARCHERS
EASY COMPANY AND THE BOOTLEGGERS
EASY COMPANY AND THE CARDSHARPS
EASY COMPANY AND THE INDIAN DOCTOR

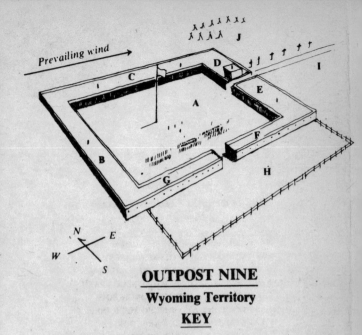

OUTPOST NINE
Wyoming Territory
KEY

A. Parade and flagstaff

B. Officers' quarters ("officers' country")

C. Enlisted men's quarters: barracks, day room, and mess

D. Kitchen, quartermaster supplies, ordnance shop, guardhouse

E. Suttler's store and other shops, tack room, and smithy

F. Stables

G. Quarters for dependents and guests; communal kitchen

H. Paddock

I. Road and telegraph line to regimental headquarters

J. Indian camp occupied by transient "friendlies"

INTERIOR . OUTSIDE

OUTPOST NUMBER NINE
(DETAIL)

Outpost Number Nine is a typical High Plains military outpost of the days following the Battle of the Little Big Horn, and is the home of Easy Company. It is not a "fort"; an official fort is the headquarters of a regiment. However, it resembles a fort in its construction.

The birdseye view shows the general layout and orientation of Outpost Number Nine; features are explained in the Key.

The detail shows a cross-section through the outpost's double walls, which ingeniously combine the functions of fortification and shelter.

The walls are constructed of sod, dug from the prairie on which Outpost Number Nine stands, and are sturdy enough to withstand an assault by anything less than artillery. The roof is of log beams covered by planking, tarpaper, and a top layer of sod. It also provides a parapet from which the outpost's defenders can fire down on an attacking force.

one _____

Nothing moved across the miles of dry grass plains. The day was empty, the far-reaching sky cloudless and oppressive. There was no wind except on those rare, unpredictable occasions when it chose to form itself into a dust devil and dance weirdly across the plains for brief moments. The sun was white in a white sky, as it had been for week upon week of endless, unendurable heat. The ground was baked to cracked, rock-hard clay. The trees along the bottoms hung their heads miserably, their foliage brown and dry. Outpost Number Nine sweltered.

Outpost Number Nine, squat against the wide stretch of the Wyoming plains, endured the heat poorly. There had been words exchanged between suffering, short-tempered men, and at least one fistfight involving the hair-triggered Private Malone and a transient enlisted man.

Private Ambrose Hollis stood on the rampart of Number Nine, standing his guard duty under these extreme, breathless conditions. Sweat trickled down his throat and chest. His uniform clung to him, He itched, his feet burned, he couldn't seem to catch his breath.

The plains swam before his eyes and he angrily consulted his pocket watch. Seven-thirty. The last thirty minutes had crept past. Holzer, his relief, wasn't due until nine. He'd be lucky if Holzer found him alive, Hollis decided.

Turning away from the gate briefly, he saw the knot of men in front of the sutler's store, guzzling beer as fast as they could hoist it, hiding in the meager shade of Pop Evans's awning. There was no laughter, very little talk that Hollis could hear. He recognized Rafferty, Stretch Dobbs, and Wojensky. They didn't seem to be having a particularly good time.

The beer cooled no one, it only gave the body a little rap on the head, enough to let a man sleep these nights when the barracks were breathless and sweat rolled off a man, soaking the bedsheets.

No, they weren't enjoying any of it very much. Still, Hollis envied them. He was standing fully exposed to the blinding sun, and his throat was as dry as Mojave sand. He turned away angrily.

Lately it had been that way—his temper was hardly under control. He, like Malone, felt like hitting someone, anyone. A wild notion to desert had flitted through his mind one desperately hot night when everyone lay snoring and stinking in the stultifying barracks.

Hollis looked again at his watch—7:35.

Jesus! He ran his sleeve across his forehead and paced slowly back and forth, his rifle slung over his shoulder. His mind, in self-defense, had begun to wander, to weave a dream world.

2

He walked beside the tropical pool, and hearing the sounds of laughter and splashing, he looked that way. A group of brown-breasted native women were playing in the water, beckoning to him. A crystal waterfall spilled from the heights, shimmering in the sunlight. He went nearer, stripping off his uniform tunic. The girl rose from out of the water...

It was Sergeant Cohen.

Angrily, Hollis spun on his heel, looking out at the brown grass plains. Nothing stirred. Someone shouted from Pop Evans's porch. Hollis didn't even glance that way. Bastards and their beer.

...she lifted a long, slender arm, and with her hands made graceful, clearly sensual gestures up over her water-glossed hips. She cupped her breasts, threw her head back, and laughed, revealing perfect white teeth and a melon-pink tongue. Hollis was naked, swimming toward her with powerful strokes; the water around him was the same temperature as his body. There was a red flower above the girl's ear, fixed into her raven-black, glossy hair. He reached her and his arms stretched out...

"Hey, Hollis!"

Private Ambrose Hollis blinked and spun around. It was Rafferty, standing uncertainly, the stink of beer on him, a grin on his broad mouth.

"What the hell do you want?" Ambrose snapped.

"Thought you might want to talk or something, Hollis. Christ, what's bothering you?"

"The heat, Rafferty. The heat is bothering me!" Hollis's words were spoken rapid-fire between clenched teeth. He could feel the grit of dust clinging to his perspiration-streaked face. "Would you mind, Rafferty—I'm not supposed to be talking to you."

"Pardon *me*," Rafferty said with evident sarcasm.

3

"Christ, please forgive me!" He waved a hand above his head and Hollis watched him turn and saunter back toward the sutler's.

Hollis stood motionless for a minute, the sun, like a merciless adversary, drilling his eyes, piercing his skull, bludgeoning him with heat and light.

. . . he was swimming toward her . . . he was reaching out toward her . . .

Dammit, it wouldn't work! The pool was only sand and sagebrush, the woman Ben Cohen, and Hollis leaned heavily against the stockade wall, wiping his eyes.

He was going to faint. He was going to faint and fall off the wall and nobody gave a damn. Three hours of guard duty—in this weather, it shouldn't be more than an hour. Anybody with common sense could see that. But the army was short on common sense.

He straightened up, squaring his hat. Mr. Taylor was duty officer, and although Hollis hadn't seen the second lieutenant peering out of the officers' quarters, it would be Hollis's luck to have him do so just then, when he was sagging against the wall, hat off.

He sighed, glanced at his watch, and trudged on. The sun was sinking lower now. It was half hidden by the distant mountains. Still, it sent probing sabers of light across the dry land. The legacy of its heat lingered.

One more hour. Twilight was settling slowly, the land was hazed with a soft purple, nearly blue in the washes. The temperature remained fixed.

It was time for the perimeter search, and Hollis let himself out through the gate. Once an hour, on the hour, the watch was required to make a circuit of the post. There was never anything there, but it was in the manual. As if a party of hostiles were hiding outside the walls. Hollis grumbled to himself as he walked the well-worn path around the outside

4

of Outpost Number Nine. His feet kicked up tiny puffs of dust with every plodding step. Nothing. There was nothing at all but scattered sage and clumps of dry buffalo grass. The shadows were growing longer, blending together, darkening the land, but there was still enough light to see.

Hollis rounded the corner of the wall, and his thoughts rambled once more.

. . . he had reached the girl. His arms encircled her, his hands running across the damp, silky flesh of this island princess. He could feel the flexing of her back muscles beneath that honey-colored flesh, the incredible strength of her hips, and she laughed, pressing against him, her firm breasts flattening against his chest. She opened her mouth and tilted her head back . . .

The shot thundered out of the twilight and ripped past Hollis's ear. It tore into the thick sod wall of the stockade, raising a plume of dust and bits of dry grass, and he hit the ground, his heart hammering, his pulse rumbling in his ears. He pressed his face to the earth for a long minute, awaiting a second shot. Then he raised his head warily, wide-eyed, his glance sweeping the plains. Nothing.

The smoke from the unseen rifle was gone. Twilight was fading rapidly to darkness and there was nothing, absolutely nothing to be seen. Still, Hollis did not move. He could see nothing, but there was a man out there with a rifle who had been able to see him, and that slug had come within inches of killing him.

Mr. Taylor, rifle in hand, burst from the officers' quarters at the sound of the shot. Looking across the parade, he could see the loafers on Pop Evans's porch making for the gate. A dozen men in various stages of undress had rushed out of the enlisted barracks with Malone, barefoot and shirtless, at their head.

"What was that?" someone shouted. Taylor didn't turn

to answer or see who was calling. Sprinting across the parade, he was already nearly to the gate.

"Where's Hollis?" Taylor asked, and Rafferty answered.

"He was making his circuit, sir. Just went out."

"Damn."

Taylor didn't hesitate. Looking around to make sure his men were armed, he led them out into the near-darkness. There was no need to caution them to be careful.

Quickly they ran along the path cut by sentries' boots, eyes searching the darkness. Malone, stubbing a bare toe on a rock, muttered a curse. They found Hollis where he had hurled himself.

Taylor moved in a crouch toward his sentry, and flattening himself out as well, he asked first: "Are you hurt?"

"No, sir." Hollis, he noticed, was trembling slightly.

"What happened?"

"Beats the hell out of me. Someone took a shot at me."

"You didn't see who?" Taylor's eyes searched the darkness. He couldn't see more than ten feet now. Twilight had evaporated, night settled in a matter of minutes.

"I couldn't see a damn thing . . . sir," Hollis added. "All I know's someone took a potshot."

"Catch sight of his smoke?" Malone asked.

"No. Nothin'," Hollis repeated.

The sound of running feet brought their heads around, and Taylor looked up to see his commanding officer, pistol in hand, moving swiftly toward them.

"What's going on here?" Warner Conway demanded.

"Someone took a shot at Private Hollis, sir," Taylor responded.

A couple of the men had come to attention, and Conway barked, "Get down!" They obliged gratefully. "See anything at all, Hollis?" the captain asked.

6

"Nothin', sir. I don't know who it was or where the shot come from."

"Hostiles?" Taylor wondered.

"Maybe." Conway peered out at the dark and empty land. His first inclination was to send a party out to find that sniper. He wouldn't tolerate having his men picked off by some sharpshooter. But he knew the thought was reckless. It was just too dark. A party of men would be easy pickings for the sniper if he felt like fighting; and if he didn't, they hadn't a chance in Hades of finding the bastard.

"Not much point in going out there, is there, sir?" Taylor asked, echoing his thoughts.

"Not tonight. But in the morning I want that area gone over inch by inch. I won't have this, Taylor."

"No, sir."

Captain Conway was smoldering, and Taylor could feel the heat. The captain was the kind of officer who hated to lose men, hated writing those letters home. At times it happened—it was a part of the life they led—but to have it sneak up out of the darkness and snatch a man's life away angered him. Conway reached out and slapped Hollis affectionately on the shoulder—an indication of how he felt, and a gesture not one officer in a hundred would make.

Then he rose, "Who's Hollis's relief, Mr. Taylor?"

"Holzer, sir."

"Tell him to watch his butt, and I mean it." Then the captain was gone, spinning on a heel, striding down the dark path.

Hollis was helped to his feet, and as he dusted himself off, the men drifted back toward the gate.

"Who do you figure?" Rafferty asked Malone.

"Some Cheyenne buck passing by. He looks up and there's Hollis, so he takes a shot."

7

"Likely."

"Unless Ambrose has got him an enemy somewhere."

They walked through the gate and headed toward the barracks, where knots of men stood holding similar discussions.

"Hollis? I don't think so," Rafferty said.

"Tell you what," Malone said, "I'm damned glad my watch duty don't come up for a while."

"What do you mean?" Rafferty asked with some anxiety. He was scheduled for tomorrow night. Malone was grinning, so he had just been giving Rafferty the needle. Still, it was something to think about. Suppose the sniper, whoever it was, just liked to shoot bluelegs?

Stamping into the barracks, they found Wolfgang Holzer pulling his highly polished boots on, surrounded by half a dozen men, all trying to explain to him what had happened and to caution him to be careful.

Wojensky's hands flew up, and he turned away in frustration.

"What's the matter, Corp?" Malone asked with a grin. "Problems with the Deutscher?"

"The same old thing. You talk to him—damned if I care if he *does* get himself shot."

Malone tried. "You heard the shot, didn't you, Wolfgang?"

"*Ja*. A shot." He nodded.

"Someone fired at Hollis. The man might still be out there, so you watch your butt tonight. We can't lose the only spit-and-polish soldier we got."

"*Ja*. A shot," Holzer repeated. Malone shrugged.

"I wish I'd started learning German the day he showed up," Wojensky said to the floor. "Because he ain't never going to learn English. Never, I know it!"

Holzer had shouldered his rifle, and now he squared his

cap. Bowing stiffly to Wojensky, he clicked his heels and went out to the gate to relieve Hollis.

Holzer did understand what everyone was trying to tell him; he'd have to have been a fool not to. The shot ringing out, the men rushing to the perimeter, returning with an obviously shaken Hollis. Holzer would have to have been a fool, and he was not. His lack of English made him seem to be a little dense. Things often had to be repeated endlessly, slowly, loudly before he understood. But a rifle shot speaks quite clearly.

He relieved Hollis and, as was required, went out himself to make a circuit. He walked slowly, his rifle ready, his thoughts on nothing but defense. Nothing.

He breathed a sigh of relief as he made the fourth corner and had the gate in sight once more. Entering, he barred the gate behind him and settled in for three hours of duty, remembering a long-ago winter in Prussia when he had frolicked in the snow with Hilda Mueller, whose cheeks were as red as apples, whose arms were soft and chubby and quite warm.

In the barracks, it would have taken more than memories of distant winters to cool things off. It had started quite innocently . . .

McBride, Malone, and Wojensky were playing poker while Trueblood shaved—he hated doing it in the morning, when he was sluggish and bleary-eyed—and the other men, in various stages of undress, lay spread against their bunks like wilted flowers. Armstrong had managed to fall asleep somehow, and his stentorian snoring racketed through the barracks.

"Pair of aces," Malone mumbled. The game didn't hold a man's interest, and he had been wondering how to wangle a pass to town from Ben Cohen. The first shirt was grouchy with the heat as well, and speaking to him was a good way to get your head torn off or get your name on the latrine-pit detail.

"Sixes and fours," Wojensky said, and raked in the pennies and nickels lethargically.

Bill Fox lay on his bunk, staring at the ceiling. He hadn't moved for hours. He might have been dead, but periodically his mouth would move and he would mutter, "Jesus, is it hot. Jesus!"

He did so now and Amos Brandt, the huge former cavalryman, responded, "Shut up, Fox."

Wojensky's eyes shuttled that way. There had been trouble between some of the men, most of it attributable to the heat, which, laid on top of the usual privations—the lack of women, of comfort, the constant danger—caused tempers to grow unusually short.

There had once been a man named Dwight DeVeers in Easy Company, a small man with a thin, cultured voice, who was totally out of place. No one ever discovered what had caused DeVeers, who was obviously well educated and presumably well fixed for money, to enlist. He had been a queer duck, aloof and brittle, but DeVeers had known quite a bit if you got him to talking.

Once, after witnessing a barracks fight, DeVeers had gotten to talking about a man named Sampson at Yale University—DeVeers talked as if he had known him personally. Sampson, it seemed was some kind of scientist.

"Doctor V. H. Sampson," Private DeVeers had advised them, "has proven with all manner of small animals that the more closely confined, the more numerous any creature is, the more likely is violence to occur among them. Add discomfort—heat, cold, lack of food—and it becomes inevitable."

Wojensky hoped that Sampson's Law wasn't at work here. He liked Bill Fox; the tall Arkansawyer did his work

10

without complaint and he had proven himself to be a fighter. Brandt had a clouded past. Once a cavalryman, he had left the army—some said under pressure—before returning two years later to mounted infantry. He was sullen and fancied himself as a brawler, although he kept his fighting image in his pocket now, since Malone had shut off his water one dark night out behind the paddock.

"Raise you six cents," Malone said. Wojensky looked at his pair of fours and went along with it. Reb McBride, holding an unlighted half-cigar between his teeth, flipped him three cards.

"Dealer folds," McBride said. "Open the door, will you?"

"Christ, it's hot!" Fox repeated.

Brandt sat up sharply, his small red eyes glaring in the direction of Fox. "We know it's hot, dammit, Fox!" he grumbled. "Nobody needs your weather reports every five minutes."

Fox lifted his eyelids and replied, "Sorry."

Brandt perched on the edge of his bunk hopefully. A good fistfight might release some of the tension. But Fox had closed his weary eyes and Brandt, still muttering, rose and walked to the door in his underwear, taking a deep breath of the outside air, which was still dry and warm. At least it was fresh. The barracks smelled of man-sweat, tobacco, and stale bedclothes.

"Three eights," Malone said, winning back exactly the amount he had lost on the last hand. "I got to get a pass," he said to McBride. The bugler yawned and stretched.

"Fat chance. With Miller's squad out with Fitzgerald, we're shorthanded now."

"Someone could lay around here and sweat double to cover for me," Malone suggested sourly. "What do you think, Wojensky?"

11

"You can try," the corporal responded. "Myself, I'd stay clear of Sergeant Cohen."

"Good advice," McBride put in. "He damned near took my head off yesterday."

"Yeah." Malone drummed his stubby, much-broken fingers on the table, which was shaped like a half moon, butted up against the wall. "Damn, I could use some whiskey and a woman."

"Don't start that talk," Trueblood said, drying his face, his shave complete.

"What talk?" Malone's head swiveled.

"Woman talk. I don't want to hear any woman talk," Trueblood said.

"Sixes and kings," McBride announced apathetically. He too was now even. "I've had enough," he said, stretching.

"Me too," Wojensky admitted.

"*Jesus*, it's hot," Bill Fox mumbled.

Amos Brandt stiffened, his huge back muscles flexing. He turned from the doorway, his fists tightly clenched. Malone nudged Wojensky with his elbow, and the corporal turned to see Brandt, sweat raining off his broad forehead, walk across the room. He went directly to where Trueblood stood drying his face, picked up Trueblood's shallow basin of water, and dumped it onto Bill Fox.

"Jesus! What in hell!" Fox sat up sharply as if propelled by springs. Brandt stood over him, his dull little eyes gleaming.

"Now maybe you're not so damned hot!" Brandt shouted.

Wojensky started to rise, but Brandt, setting the bowl aside, walked back to his bunk and crawled in. Fox watched him go, his eyes uncomprehending at first, then slowly changing from mirrors of unhappiness to smoldering coals of anger. Gradually, Fox's tense face relaxed and the anger went out of his eyes. A distant amusement seemed to take its place and he lay back.

Malone and McBride exchanged a look and a shrug. There would be no fight at least, and so they wandered to their own bunks, flopping down on the thin mattresses to pass an unpleasant night.

The post had quieted. The men in front of Pop Evans's had cleared out, returning to the barracks. Pop's lanterns were now out, as were the lamps around the barracks. Captain Warner Conway had been standing at the window for most of an hour since entering the commanding officer's quarters. Now, satisfied that Holzer had made his circuit unmolested, he dropped the curtain and turned from the window. She lay abed, watching him with dark, eager eyes.

"Everything all right, dear?" Flora Conway asked. Her voice was as warm and sultry as the day had been.

"Apparently." Warner Conway sat on the chair, removed his boots with the aid of a boot jack, sighed, and began unbuttoning his tunic. Flora watched him with great interest.

"How is Lieutenant Dunwoodie doing?"

"Adequately. He's itching to get on to Cheyenne, but with Fitzgerald and Kincaid both gone, I can't let him go yet."

"Poor Matt," the captain's lady said sympathetically, but her eyes and thoughts were on Warner Conway as he stepped from his trousers, and not on the absent Lieutenant Matt Kincaid.

"Poor Matt?" Conway walked naked across the room, lifted the chimney from the lamp, and blew out the flame. "Fitzgerald and Taylor were green with envy, thinking of Matt riding off to that sin-ridden town. I know you hate to think of it, Flora, but our junior officers are somewhat

13

amenable to the suggestions of vice."

"And you, Warner?" she asked, throwing back the sheet so that he could slip in beside her, warm, sinewy, masculine.

"Only to vices of a restricted and singular nature."

"Meaning?" she cooed, rolling toward him to be wrapped into his strong arms.

"Meaning"—he kissed her nose—"that not only do I love you, woman, but I am passionately devoted to your still rather lush body and its pleasures."

"Are you?" she teased.

"Of course."

She took his hand and guided it to her breast. "Don't you think that maybe I'm starting to lose a little there? Sag, grow less firm."

Obviously Warner Conway didn't, or couldn't have cared. His hand caressed the globe of her breast, marveling at the soft fullness. His mouth crept nearer and toyed with the taut nipple as Flora's hand stroked the back of his head.

"Excellent condition, all quite excellent."

She kissed his lips and guided his hand downward between the soft warmth of her thighs. "That," she asked, her voice breathy and humid. "Would you say that's in prime shape as well? It's often used. Perhaps..."

Conway's fingers dipped into the warm crevice and he slowly stroked her, finding her wet, eager. He rolled to her hungrily.

"Woman, you are a fool. The equipment is obviously peerless and priceless." He kissed her, felt her hand linger on his chest and then drop down slowly to encircle his erection.

"Peerless and priceless," she breathed into his ear. "You too, Warner, are peerless and priceless."

"Enough games?" he asked, his voice rather dry.

"Yes. Enough." She rolled away from him and her legs

slowly spread, her arms slowly drew him down, and Warner followed eagerly.

Her arms were around his shoulders, her lips on his chest and throat, lips and cheek. He stroked the inner side of her thigh, marveling at its texture, at the muscle tone beneath the silky flesh, and then again his fingers dipped inside her.

Flora's head lolled back against the pillow and her eyes, half closed, reflected soft pleasure. She slid a hand down across her own abdomen to find Warner's erection. She held it for a moment, amazed at the rush of surprise and anticipation which flooded through her. Then, gently, she took the head of his shaft and positioned it, inviting his peerless and priceless equipment to enter.

Enter he did, sliding slowly in, the tender warmth of Flora Conway's body encasing him deliciously. Her breath came in a series of gasps now, and her hands roamed his flanks, clenching his hard-muscled buttocks.

She held him still in her for a moment, feeling the pulsing of his body, the throbbing of her own heart, the slow adjustments her body made to his, the increased dampness of her peerless and priceless equipment—for just a moment before he began to thrust against her and she responded eagerly, her hips taking on a life of their own as she swayed and rolled, pitching her pelvis against his, feeling the tingling beginnings of a deep and most satisfactory climax.

She reached it almost instantly, surprising her husband with the ferocity of it, her hands gripping his shoulders and then his buttocks savagely as she rolled her head from side to side and, in a gasping, voiceless plea, urged him on.

Drained, she lay back, feeling his rugged presence climbing over her, his familiar, rough hands sweeping over her breasts and flanks, tangling themselves in her hair. She felt the warmth of his breath against her throat, the teasing of his lips at her nipples, and she felt her body responding,

15

rising to a second orgasm as Warner murmured to her.

Conway's temples throbbed, his loins ached. He dug at her, pressing himself against her soft flesh, burying himself inside her. He was a hungry man, and she was every delicacy imaginable. Her breasts satisfied his hunger, yet caused new hungers to develop. He was insatiable as he rocked against her, feeling her fingers drop to his crotch, to touch him as he entered her. Her soft smile was an invitation to gorge himself on her flesh, to devour her, and he buried himself to the hilt time and again, her hands, the quiet musical sounds she made deep in her throat urging him on.

He felt her begin to tremble again, felt an echoing trembling begin in his loins, and he tensed, holding himself rigid, motionless, as a deep climax drained his body. Then he lay against her, stroking her flesh, listening to her softly murmured words, wondering again what he had ever done to deserve such a woman.

"Utterly peerless," he whispered to his wife. "Utterly peerless and absolutely priceless."

two ─────────────────────────

"Malone." A hand shook the soldier out of his obscure dream. He clawed at his eyes and sat up.

It was still dark in the barracks, still warm. Malone could see only the silhouette of the man bending over him. "What?"

"Mr. Taylor's outside. He wants you."

"Wojensky?" he asked, peering at the dark figure.

"Yes."

"What time is it?"

"Four-thirty."

"Why don't you go out and tell Mr.-be-damned-Taylor to go straight to hell for me."

But already Malone's feet were on the floor. He sat there, head hanging, tongue raw and rough, circulation choked down to a near standstill, his stomach feeling sour and bloated.

"What's up?" Malone asked.

"I don't know. All I know's he wants you. Better shake out."

"Yeah. I'm shaking," Malone said. He hadn't moved. His hair hung across his eyes. The old injury to his knee was kicking up, throbbing dully. Had to be a soldier, he thought sourly.

"Malone?"

"I'm up, I'm shaking!"

Someone rolled over in his sleep and muttered. Wojensky moved away from his bunk, and Malone slowly got to his feet, staggering to the washbasin, dragging his pants behind him. Amos Brandt was snoring his head off and recalling what he had done the night before to Bill Fox. Malone considered the advisability of dumping a basin of water on the big man's head. He decided against it. There wasn't time to finish a fight.

He dressed slowly, his arms and legs wooden. He swore for the twentieth time that month that he would cut down on the sutler's lousy three-point-two beer.

He groped his way through the noisome dimness of the barracks, nearly tripping over Reb McBride, who was digging for a boot under his bunk.

McBride was the company bugler, and he was used to this predawn stuff. He had to be first up to blow reveille, something Reb seemed only occasionally to dislike.

Malone started to topple, and felt McBride's hand steady him as the corporal asked: "Malone?"

"Yeah."

"Where you going?"

"Out."

Malone wasn't known for being communicative in the

18

morning. Reb let him go. Malone staggered out the door, planting his hat. The air was fresh, but the warmth of the previous day hadn't entirely dissipated. It would be another long damned scorcher of a day, another hot night. Mr. Taylor stood beside his horse, looking crisp, although his eyes seemed a little weary.

"Morning, sir," Malone said, managing a reasonable salute.

"Malone."

"Something up?"

"I'm going out to look for that sniper's sign. Windy's off post, so I thought of you."

"I'm no Windy Madalian, sir," Malone answered. Once he had pulled Taylor out of a tough spot with a bit of lucky tracking, and apparently the lieutenant had recalled it when trying to come up with a substitute for Windy Mandalian, who had been dispatched to show a wagon train of greeners the pass through the mountains.

That was the army for you, Malone thought, do something right one time and you paid for it forever. It was like volunteering—do it once and they expected a repeat. Malone never volunteered; he had been around too long.

"I'm afraid you'll miss breakfast," Taylor said, "but maybe Dutch has some coffee boiling."

Taylor's voice indicated what kind of answer he would prefer, and so Malone gave it to him: "That's all right, sir. I'll catch up later. Let me get a horse and we'll have us a look-see, though I'd feel better if Windy was here."

Malone walked through the deep violet haze of predawn and found his way to the paddock. No one was around at this hour, so he chose and saddled a black-tailed, hammer-headed bay he favored.

The animal was ornery, given to nipping at its rider's legs, but Malone liked it. Some of the others said it was because the horse's personality was like Malone's. Actually he favored it because it was a tough, fast little horse with plenty of bottom. Out on patrol, Malone liked to keep a fast, long-running horse under him. A man never knew how far or how fast he would have to ride.

Today would require neither speed nor endurance, but he had grown attached to the stubborn, mean son of a bitch. Maybe, he reflected, they were right—he and the horse were two of a kind. Scarred, stubborn, and tough.

"Let's go, baby," Malone said to the horse. It tried to bite him as he cinched up, and he slapped the muzzle away automatically. "You'll get fat standin' around."

There was a faint, pale gray shading along the eastern horizon as Malone returned, mounted. Stars still clung to the sky. McBride hadn't come out of the barracks yet as Taylor and Malone rode through the gate and out onto the shadowed plains.

Malone looked ahead without a lot of confidence at the miles of bald prairie, broken only by sage and brown grass. "Don't seem like there's much concealment out there for a sniper," Malone commented.

"It may have been a mounted Indian who's long gone. Most probably it was. But the captain wants this checked out. If we can find some tracks or a cartridge case, it might tell us something."

"Yes, sir," Malone said without enthusiasm. They rode to the spot where the bullet had hit the stockade wall and examined it, learning nothing. The bullet had dug its way far into the wall and hit an embedded stone, and was now unidentifiable as to caliber or type.

"All I can suggest to you is that you search from this spot, using this for the point of a wedge. Fan out from side to side, swinging wider as you get farther from the post. After you get out three or four hundred yards, there's not

20

much point in going any farther, do you think?"

"No, sir." Malone wasn't sure there was much point in any of this, but he kept his mouth shut. Reveille sounded sharp and clear as dawn sketched a brilliant gold line along the dark horizon.

"I've got to get back for rollcall," Taylor said. "I'll tell Sergeant Cohen to scratch you off whatever duty roster you're on."

"Yes, sir." Malone rubbed his eyes, glanced to the skies, and saluted as Taylor swung away, walking his horse back toward the gate.

Then, with a heavy sigh, Malone slowly began to walk the recalcitrant bay from side to side, moving out in a fan-shaped pattern, his eyes alert, hoping that the bastard, whoever he was, wasn't still lurking out there.

He placed a hand on the butt of his Schofield pistol, finding it reassuringly solid and cool to the touch. He slid it up and down in his holster, assuring himself it was free. He had long ago cut the flap away, the day he saw George Powers pawing desperately at his holster while a Cheyenne renegade rode up to him and shot him in the face.

The sun was peering over the horizon, casting long shadows before the sagebrush. Already it was warm. Malone unbuttoned his shirt and continued to ride in his pattern. A hundred yards out he crossed the path of six ponies. All were unshod, probably friendlies headed for the tipi town across the deadline. The tracks were days old, crisscrossed with the tracks of insects.

Still, he paralleled them for a way, finding no sign of anyone's having dismounted, no cartridge.

A shallow wash opened up before him, and Malone dipped into it, riding along the sandy, trackless bottom for a way until he decided he was too far back for anyone to have seen Hollis, let alone potshoot him.

21

The sun rose and the sweat began to trickle down Malone's neck. He needed a cup of coffee, or a drink. His eyes blurred, his skin prickled with the heat. He was out two hundred yards or so and he stepped down, letting the horse graze on the dry grass while he walked back and forth, eyes riveted to the parched earth. He tried to figure out how much area there was to cover at four hundred yards, but his math wasn't strong enough. All he knew was that a man had very little chance of finding a single casing out here. It was going to be a long, dry day, and Malone almost wished he was out digging that latrine pit . . .

The neighbor's grass always seems greener, and Rafferty, Fox, and Brandt, who were digging the latrine pit and had Malone in sight, wished that Taylor had roused them to try some tracking.

The earth was baked solid. The picks cut shallow, clearly defined grooves in the earth, instead of caving it in. The shovelsful of earth grew heavier as the sun rose higher. Bill Fox peeled off his shirt.

"What the hell has Malone got that I ain't?" he asked no one in particular. He leaned back briefly against the side of the pit, watching the broad, sweat-glossed back of Amos Brandt as he took his turn swinging the pick. "Jesus, it's hot," Fox said.

Brandt's pick halted in mid-arc and he shot a dark, menacing glance at Fox.

"Don't say that, Fox. Please, don't say that again."

"Or what?" Fox challenged. "You'll throw another pan of water on me? I haven't forgotten that, Brandt."

Brandt's muscles were actually twitching. It was hot and airless in the waist-high pit. A drop of sweat dripped from the tip of Brandt's nose.

Rafferty lifted his eyes to the heavens and sighed. Why

in hell did he have to draw duty with these two? He stepped between them.

"Let me take a shift with that pick, Amos."

Rafferty's hand closed on the pick handle, and Brandt reluctantly relinquished it. Fox and Brandt stood motionless, eyeing each other—measuring, perhaps. Amos Brandt was a head taller than Fox and easily thirty pounds heavier, but Fox had a wiry, competent-looking frame. His chin jutted forward defiantly.

Rafferty swung the pick overhead, and both men had to step aside. From the corner of his eye he saw Brandt grab his shirt and clamber out of the pit.

"Where are you going, Brandt?" he asked, wiping the sweat from his eyes.

"Over to the old latrine," Brandt said sourly, "unless you want me to start this one right now."

"What a bastard," Fox said after Brandt had gone. "And if he thinks I'll forget that water, he's crazy."

"Let it alone, Bill, just let it alone."

"Like hell."

"It's hot. Everyone's a little crazy just now," Rafferty said.

"If he thinks I'll forget that . . ."

Rafferty turned to look at Bill Fox. Fox's eyes were oddly glazed. The cords of his neck stood out tautly. He looked half mad.

"Have a drink, Bill. Cool off."

But Fox didn't answer; he stood looking at the spot where Brandt had vanished, and then, incredibly, a slow, devious smile began to spread across his mouth.

"Let's get this done and get out of here," Fox said with sudden cheerfulness. He picked up a shovel and began heaving the earth from the pit. Rafferty watched him warily for a moment, wondering if the heat hadn't caused something to snap, but Fox was whistling happily as he worked and Rafferty, shrugging mentally, put his back into his own work.

Malone gave it up at noon. He crouched in the shade of his horse, mopping his face with his scarf. He had seen nothing—no tracks of man or horse, no suspiciously flattened grass, no brass cartridge, no threads clinging to the brush. Nothing. Zero.

"If there's anything out here to be found, it'll take a better man than I am to find it," he muttered.

In response, the horse tried to bite Malone's ear off. Standing, Malone stepped into leather, turning the bay back toward the post through the shimmering heat of the day. It had long ago passed a hundred degrees. The sun hung motionless in the white sky, taunting them.

Someone had come out of the post an hour earlier and mercifully called the latrine pit crew in before someone died of heatstroke.

Malone tied up his horse, and dusting himself off with his hat, he stomped into the orderly room. Corporal Four Eyes Bradshaw, bent over a stack of ruled yellow papers, nearly leaped out of his seat. First Sergeant Ben Cohen looked up miserably. It was an oven in the orderly room. Cohen looked like a heat-dazed ox, ready to gore anything that came near.

"Afternoon, Sergeant," Malone said. Four Eyes jittered something onto the floor and Cohen's eyes swept that way.

"What is it, Malone?"

"Mr. Taylor around? I'm supposed to report to him."

"He went over to the Indian agency. Captain's in."

None of Cohen's words were antagonistic, but he delivered them choppily, his teeth nearly clenched. Cohen had his sleeves rolled up, and sweat glistened on his massive

24

forearms. He had a mad on, but not against Malone or anybody else in particular. He was simply mad. Mad at the day, the world.

Malone pulled his shirt free of the perspiration on his chest. Then, with a nod, he went to the commanding officer's door and rapped twice.

"Come in." Captain Conway's voice was cracked and a little sullen. It was no cooler in his office than it was in the orderly room.

Malone managed a wilted salute, which the captain answered. His look seemed to urge Malone to say whatever he had come to say and then get out.

Malone did so. "Mr. Taylor had me scouting for sign of that sniper, sir. Couldn't turn anything up."

"Did you go over the ground carefully?"

"Inch by inch, sir."

"Damn it, there should have been something."

Malone's jaw muscles clenched slightly. Sweat trickled down his spine. "I couldn't find a thing, sir," he repeated a little stiffly.

"All right." Conway sagged back into his chair, waving a hand, which Malone took for his cue to exit. He saluted and crept from the room. Conway had his own mad on.

He closed the door behind him and looked at the tense form of Ben Cohen. Perspiration trickled from the first sergeant's face, spotting the paper he was reading. His face was molded into a stony scowl. Malone took a deep breath and tried to form a smile.

"You know, Sarge, I—"

"No passes!" Cohen thundered, and Malone winced. Turning sharply away, he went out of the oven of the orderly room and into the furnace of the day.

Malone put up his horse and returned to the barracks. Sagging onto his bunk, he stared at the ceiling and lay inert as the sweat rivuleted off his body.

"Malone!" The voice was urgent, and Malone glanced toward the door. It was Bill Fox, and he drew a growling response.

"What the hell to you want?"

"Watch this!"

Malone's eyes narrowed with vague curiosity. Fox closed the barracks door almost all the way, so that only eight or nine inches of white, searing light showed. Then, dragging a chair over to the door, he climbed onto it, hoisting something over his head.

"What in hell are you doing, Fox? The sun baked your brains, has it?"

"Just watch." Fox put a finger to his lips and backed away from the door. After a minute, Malone heard the heavy clomping of boots on the boardwalk, and the door swung open.

As it opened, Malone saw the broad, red face of Amos Brandt, and then the bucket that Fox had balanced on top of the door.

Brandt had started to say something to Malone, but whatever it was drowned out. A gallon of water hit Brandt's head and shoulders, drenching him, washing his hair over his eyes. The bucket, tauntingly, clanged off his skull and rattled to the floor.

Brandt stood motionless. His hands were clenched and he began slowly and methodically to curse everything in nature's cornucopia. He hadn't gotten far when the convulsive laughter penetrated his rage and he looked up to see Bill Fox, nearly doubled up with amusement, howling maniacally.

"By God, Fox!" he bawled. He started forward, slipped on a patch of wet floor, and went down with a jarring thud.

Brandt roared in pain, and Fox laughed until the tears rolled from his eyes.

Brandt got to his feet like an awakening Titan, and Fox sobered a little. Brandt walked slowly forward and then lunged at the smaller soldier, but Fox neatly sidestepped him, leaped over a bunk and then another, and was out the door, still hooting with laughter.

"By God, I'll kill him. I'll tear his heart out, Malone! You hear me?"

Brandt sat down on his bunk and, shaking his massive head from side to side like a bull buffalo on the prod, resumed his cursing.

Grub call sounded and Malone gratefully swung from his bunk, grabbing his hat as he walked to the door, the mumblings of Amos Brandt in his ears.

McBride was outside, hands on hips. He glanced at Malone.

"What's going on?" Reb wanted to know.

"What do you mean?"

"I just saw Bill Fox come out of the barracks and go leaping across parade, waving his hands like a raving maniac."

Malone told him, and Reb, striding with Malone toward the grub hall, said, "Someone's going to get killed if this heat doesn't break." He glanced at the sky, squinting at the fierce ball of the sun. "Someone's surely going to get killed."

three ————————————————

The horses drank from the cold-running Belle Fourche River, twitching their tails with satisfaction. The men sat in the dry shade beneath the willows, watching the glimmering flats and the stark bulk of Devil's Tower silhouetted against the blue-white sky. Matt Kincaid mopped his throat with his scarf and removed his hat, running his fingers through his dark, perspiration-damp hair.

Cicadas hummed in the willow brush and a mockingbird darted through the trees, chasing insects. Gus Olsen's face was red with heat and exhaustion, Private Aaron Shy looked no better. Matt wondered how he looked himself—beat, he supposed. They had the right to look beat. No breeze stirred along the riverbottom, and although it should have been cooler there, they couldn't feel it.

"Let's take a swim, men," Matt suggested, and Shy must have been waiting for his lieutenant to do so. He was up and out of his uniform in less than a minute, walking to the shallow Belle Fourche. Gus Olsen saw Shy go in with a shallow dive. Then the private yelled, "Damn! It's cold!"

"Can't complain about that," Olsen called back. He was slowly stripping off his own uniform, and in another minute he was in the waist-high water beside Shy. Matt Kincaid was with them shortly.

The horses stood looking with wide-eyed appraisal at the three men whose white shoulders and chests appeared above the water.

"Great," Olsen said with satisfaction. "Think we can wade downstream to Monument?"

"It's an idea," Matt responded. He dipped his head under the icy water of the Belle Fourche and rose, chilled. But the almighty sun dried his shoulders and back within seconds. Hot gusts of wind whipped the moisture away.

Aaron Shy, seated now in the river, only his sharp, dark face protruding, commented, "I think this is all a wild-goose chase anyway, sir. Hell, I know this area and there ain't no town around here."

"There wasn't," Matt agreed, "but there's supposed to be now. God knows what we'll find. The telegram said that there had been a gold strike and a boom-town had sprung up. And according to our information, there's blood flowing in the streets. I hope the report is exaggerated, because if it's not, we're going to have to establish martial law, and we've got better uses for Easy Company than patrolling a gold-mad boomtown."

"Still don't believe it," Shy said. "There's no gold up in this area and everyone knows it."

"Apparently there are a few men who don't know it,"

Matt replied. The private fell silent, shrugging his submerged shoulders.

"Maybe they've all packed up and gone home," Sergeant Olsen said hopefully.

"We can hope so," Matt said. He looked around, and then told them with a sigh, "I guess we'd better get moving. Picnic's over, men."

After dressing, they saddled up and turned northward, following the river. Within minutes they were as hot as ever. Dust rose from the horses' plodding hooves. The sun beat down, battering their senses. Kincaid glanced at the northern skies, hoping for some sign of a change in the weather, but there wasn't the slightest wisp of cloud. His uniform was stuck to his body. Insects plagued his ears, nose, and eyes. The riverbottom was airless and still.

It was late afternoon when they dragged out of the bottom, crested the low, barren hills, and suddenly came upon it.

Monument was no myth. The town had indeed sprung up in this wilderness, and after mile upon mile of empty plains it almost seemed a mirage, albeit a jumbled, slovenly mirage.

There were half a dozen new false-fronted buildings in various stages of completion, but the majority of the town was composed of tents and shacks. Some of the tents had wooden siding, and the shacks were constructed of whatever was at hand—tarpaper, old lumber, untrimmed logs, mud, and brush. The hillsides above and beyond the town were cluttered with camps. In the main street of Monument, actually its only street, hundreds of horses milled or were tied to hitch rails before the largest buildings—the saloons.

"Well," Gus Olsen said quietly, "it don't look too bad. I don't see blood running in the streets."

31

They had to get closer for that. They rode down off the hills, a dry rising wind in their faces, and slowly the town took on life. They could hear hammers banging as a new liquor emporium was hastily constructed, hear the shrieks of women, the laughter of men. Walking their horses up the street, they saw a cowboy lying drunk or dead in the middle of the thoroughfare, traffic detouring around him. A gunshot sounded somewhere close by, and a man in overalls staggered from the front door of a saloon, holding his chest. He turned, walked three steps, and folded up, falling against the dirt of the street. No one came out to see what had happened. Gus Olsen swung down and rushed to the man.

He turned him over and glanced up at Kincaid, wagging his head. "Dead, sir."

Kincaid could hardly hear his sergeant's words above the noise of the saloon, the shouts in the street, the rumbling of wagons. Glancing upward, he saw three women in various stages of undress hanging from an upstairs window.

"Oh, soldier boy!"

"Wanta see some more, General?" This one freed a massive, flaccid breast from her chemise and displayed it to Kincaid.

"Soldier!"

A trio of drunken miners in a runaway wagon hurtled down the street directly toward Kincaid and Shy. No one had the reins, and as the wagon hit a bad chuckhole in the street, one miner flew from the wagon to land sprawled in the dirt and horse apples. The others, cheering and catcalling, rode past in a whirlwind of dust.

Olsen had mounted again, and the sergeant was grimlipped. "Why the hell do people put up with this? Why do they want to live like this? The stupid bastards."

Kincaid didn't answer. He had his own theories about

32

the master species, a part of which declared that man, of all creatures on God's earth, was the least able to tolerate freedom. It was a cynical view, perhaps, but he had Monument as evidence.

Aaron Shy was silent as they rode the length of the street. Silent because he was scared. Kincaid recognized his fear, but said nothing. Only those who were out of their senses with liquor could help being scared in this town. Men with guns walked the streets, shooting whatever or whoever they pleased. There was no law, no medical help, no order whatsoever. They were here to grow rich, one way or another. The miners dreamed of a big strike, the gamblers and holdup artists had their plans for emptying the miners' pockets. The brothel girls had their own schemes, as did the saloons and the astonishingly high-priced eateries.

It was a sin-ridden, bloody, gold-lusting town, and Kincaid cared for none of it.

At the end of the street they found a newly constructed, unpainted frame building with an amateurishly lettered sign proclaiming it a hotel, and Kincaid swung down. Followed by the two enlisted men, he went into the building, which had a packed-earth floor and a low ceiling.

Scraps of lumber were stacked in the corner near an iron stove. Coal-oil lanterns suspended from wires served as illumination. Rows of cots lined the single room that Matt could see. On the cots, several drunken miners snored.

A puncheon table set to one side seemed to be the desk, and Matt walked to it, looking for a clerk. One appeared after an interval, a fat, stocky man without much hair.

"Lieutenant," he said with some vague mockery twisting his small mouth. "Beds? Or did you lose someone? Is there a deserter among us?"

"Not to my knowledge," Kincaid said with deliberate stiffness. "My men and I need accommodations."

"Plenty of room . . ."

"Not down here. If these cots are all you have, we'll sleep out."

"I've got rooms upstairs," the clerk said. The mockery had gone from his tone, and suspicion seemed to have taken its place. "Is this government money you're spending for private rooms?" he asked. "I'm a taxpayer too, you know."

"If you've got a room for us, say so. If you don't, we'll leave."

"Hostile, aintcha? This ain't the army, Lieutenant." He shrugged one shoulder and nodded. "I got a room."

Shy had been looking the hotel over. He wasn't so sure he wanted to stay here after all. Maybe camping out was preferable to sleeping in a hole like this. It was stale and sour. The slack-jawed, whistling snores of men rang out. The barracks at Number Nine was homey by comparison.

It was the dirt, he decided. The barracks was at least kept clean. Here he saw whiskey bottles on the floor, garbage, and filthy linen. But the lieutenant had already paid and they trekked upstairs, using a staircase that had no railing.

Walking down a rough-planked corridor, they found their room. There was no key, only a drawstring. Entering, they found three cots, a plank table, and a glassless window that looked out on the street.

"Civilization," Gus Olsen said darkly. He tossed his gear beside one of the cots.

"Beg pardon, sir," Shy said to Kincaid, who stood at the open window, watching the town of Monument froth and boil, "but why exactly are we staying here at all? I mean, I thought we were supposed to investigate and report back. It's obvious already that this town needs cleaning up, and that it's the army who'll have to do it."

"It is," Matt said, turning from the window. He sailed his hat onto his cot. "But I'd like to see if something can't be done short of bringing in a squad of men. We have other uses for those soldiers, Private Shy."

What was the lieutenant planning? Shy hoped he didn't have some idea of turning the three of them into lawmen or some such thing. He understood Kincaid's logic, but he couldn't see what else was to be done.

Gus Olsen didn't either, but he had been in the army long enough not to ask. He seriously hoped Kincaid did have some idea of what he was up to, because Olsen knew one thing with certainty—if the army was brought in, the battle raging in the streets of Monument would turn into full-scale war.

With Kincaid's approval, they turned in for a little rest. Olsen thought the bedbugs were a little greedy, but he managed to nap until dark, when Kincaid shook him out. Shy was already dressing before the sundown-lighted window.

"Let's see if they've got someplace in this hellhole where a man can get a decent meal, Sergeant."

Monument by day was a peaceful, quiet village compared to Monument by night. All of the hundreds of prospectors who had been working throughout the day had apparently swooped down upon the town, swelling the raucous population. Women shrieked from the rooftops, and there was the sound of breaking glass. A cowbody hooted off down the street, riding his pony backwards until he rounded a corner, toppled out of the saddle, and lay still in an alley.

Three men were pushing and shouting at each other in the center of the street. A frowzy, half-dressed blonde stood nearby, egging them on.

The three soldiers shouldered through the miners who were clustered on the boardwalks. Eventually they found a restaurant. A sign said, "WIPE YOUR BOOTS!" and Kincaid commented, "This is obviously a classy place. Mind your manners."

They stumped inside, finding the place half empty. It wasn't the supper hour in Monument. There was time for eating after the saloons closed—if they ever did.

They seated themselves at a long table where only one other customer was eating—a grizzled, bearded, dirty prospector who didn't even look up from his tin plate. He chewed loudly, wetly, not stopping until his beard was soaked with gravy and he had sopped up the last of his food with a crust of bread. Then he rose hurriedly and walked away, not even looking at the soldiers.

Kincaid was still waiting for someone to come and take their orders when a woman in a filthy blue apron shuffled to the table balancing three tin plates and gripping a half-gallon granite coffeepot with a dishrag.

She slapped a plate down in front of each of them and upturned three of the tin cups that awaited customers, filling them with black coffee.

The plates held beef and beans, cornbread and greens.

"Good thing the lady's a mind-reader," Gus said sullenly.

"Look, soldier," she snapped back, "that's what we got. You want it, eat. You don't, I'll take it back."

"Thank you," Kincaid said, and the waitress, casting her watery blue eyes on the young officer, smiled and nodded.

"You're welcome. Always a pleasure to serve a *gentleman*." Her gaze shifted witheringly to Gus Olsen. Then she flounced off, wiping her hands on the dishrag.

"What did I say?" Gus asked with a laugh. Shy didn't answer; he was already digging in. He had expected more from the hotel and the meal, but nevertheless, he was hungry and it was hot. Kincaid didn't answer either, but his reasons were entirely different.

Reasons, there were two. A minor reason and a major one. The minor reason was the man in a neat dark gray suit who had just entered the restaurant and now stood looking over the room. The major reason was the dark-haired, blue-eyed woman at his elbow.

Young she was, beautiful and animated. Her eyes flickered to Matt's, made brief, challenging contact, and flitted away again. She said something to the man beside her, and he too looked at Kincaid. Then together they started across the room toward the table where Matt sat before his untouched plate.

"Lieutenant?"

Olsen's head came around, as did that of Aaron Shy. Shy did a quick double take upon seeing the woman. Matt rose.

"Yes?"

"I'm Christopher Lacklander. My daughter, Marie."

"Matt Kincaid," he replied. He took the man's gnarled, leathery hand and asked, "Is there something I can do for you?"

"I don't . . . can we talk?" Lacklander said, looking over his shoulder and then at the two enlisted men.

"Of course. Please." Matt gestured toward the bench, and as they seated themselves, he studied the woman again. At close quarters she was even prettier. Her dark hair was curled and stacked on her small skull, revealing small pink ears. Her eyes were pale, pale blue, nearly gray, and they were shrewdly intelligent. She caught Matt appraising her and smiled noncommittally, folding her hands in her lap.

"We were hoping," Lacklander began, "that the army might move in to this small-scale Gomorrah of ours. Sixteen men killed in six weeks, sir." He read something in Kincaid's eyes. "That is your purpose—to maintain order in Monument?"

37

"Not exactly, sir. I have been ordered to observe and report. If the lawlessness warrants military intervention, then—"

"If it warrants it!" Lacklander said excitedly. "Did you walk over here with your eyes closed?"

"If it warrants it," Matt resumed without showing any irritation, "then a party of soldiers will be dispatched from Outpost Number Nine. In the meantime I intend to look into alternate solutions."

"Alternate solutions?" Lacklander slapped his forehead in amazement. "Do you know, sir, that my daughter cannot walk the streets of this town, that my claim has twice been placed under siege by claim-jumpers, that decent people are helpless in Monument? What alternate solution can there possibly be?"

"Several possibilities suggest themselves," Matt said. He looked at the girl and was surprised to find her eyes liquid and distant. He quickly returned his gaze to Lacklander's face. "It is costly and inconvenient to shift army forces to Monument. Our men are needed on the plains, Mister Lacklander. What Monument needs is local law. I would like to see a strong town marshal installed, or failing that, to see committee law—"

"Vigilantes!" Lacklander scoffed. "I've seen vigilante law in Kansas—they get rid of the outlaws all right, and kill off half the good people in the process. When they're done, you're left with a pack of men no better than the ones they strung up."

"If chosen carefully—" Matt was again cut off by Lacklander.

"There aren't six men in Monument who are decent and gun-wise both. I know, I've already tried exactly what you suggest."

"I mean to try again, sir," Matt said, his manner a bit

more stiff. "Monument's problem should be handled by local people. Even if the army does come in—which we are trying to avoid, if at all possible—where will you stand when the army pulls out again? The same elements will drift back once the soldiers are gone."

Lacklander was silent for a moment, his mouth drawn down. Finally, with a shake of his head, he answered, "You know, Lieutenant, you're right. Damn me if you're not. It's just that a man looks for an easy solution. Look, I did try to organize a vigilante group, but the sort of men we've got here . . . well, they came to get rich quick and get out quicker. They don't give a damn if we've got hell on earth down here, as long as they can buy beans and whiskey and get back to their diggings. Truth is, I feel the same way."

"But you care, Daddy," the girl said, speaking for the first time. Her voice was nicely modulated, more cultured than Matt had expected. She placed a hand on her father's sleeve. "My father tried, Lieutenant Kincaid. The trouble is, there aren't enough others who care. Let anything go on—that's their attitude—as long as it doesn't touch them personally. And when it does!" she laughed. "How they cry then, when it's too late.'"

"Look." Christopher Lacklander spoke in an undertone. He inclined his head slightly toward the door, and Matt's eyes followed the gesture.

A big man in a filthy tweed coat and dark pants stood in the doorway of the restaurant, returning Matt's gaze. He was redheaded, mustached, and whiskered. With a prominent, broad forehead and a receding chin, he looked dull and quite dangerous.

"Someone I should know?" Matt asked.

"Someone no one should know," Marie snapped. "That's Murray Hill. He's one of that Diamond Glen mob."

Matt had noticed a saloon with that name, and he asked

if that was what she referred to.

"Yes. The Diamond Glen saloon crowd. Frank Toomey is the owner of the saloon and the leader of these ruffians." Marie's eyes sparked now with anger, and Matt glanced again at the big man, who smiled mockingly and walked to the back of the restaurant, taking a corner table.

"Toomey, Murray Hill, and a bunch of others drifted in together from the Black Hills, Lieutenant," Lacklander told Matt. "Got run out is what I think must've happened. They sell whiskey other men wouldn't sell to an Indian, and there've been men go into the Diamond Glen who never came out. Out in the hills, anything can happen and often does, and it's generally Toomey who's behind it—at least so a man suspicions. Proving it—well, I wouldn't think it could be proved. Take China Tyler—he had a claim out near me, but it's an isolated spot. A man is found dead in the hills. Who saw anything? Nobody. If anyone did, no one's saying nothing. What are they going to do? Accuse Toomey to his face?"

Matt muttered sympathetic sounds. It was true, they had a bad situation here and it was bound to get worse. That lure of gold was likely to bring half the outlaws, pickpockets, prostitutes, and cardsharps in the territory to Monument. Most of those people followed the gold from one boomtown to the next, leaving when the gold ran out or the town suggested it. Finding gold was no task at all compared to trying to keep it.

"What are most of the miners doing about protecting their dust, Mr. Lacklander? I assume it's dust—there's no hardrock mining yet, is there?"

"No. Panning, cradling, hydraulicking..."

"Whereabouts, mostly?" Private Shy asked. "I been through this country plenty. I hate to think I was riding right past that gold and never seeing a thing."

40

"Mostly up along Danby Creek, that's where it all started."

"Danby, huh?" Shy said. He nodded and fell silent, pouring himself another cup of coffee. He was also looking covetously at Kincaid's untouched plate, and Matt slid it over to him.

"Is it every man for himself?" Matt asked. "Or have you tried to form some kind of banking association? What about shipping the gold?"

Lacklander hesitated, spread his hands, and said with a dry laugh, "I guess it's every man for himself. Actually, to be honest, I haven't had to—"

"My father's claim hasn't panned out," Maria said quickly. "Not that it won't, of course. We know the gold's up there, it's just that we haven't had enough gold to worry about."

"I see." Matt sipped his own coffee. "Who has the richest claims up there?"

"Well..." Lacklander looked at his daughter. "Clive Scales, I guess, would be one. He was one of the first men in here. And George Bestwick."

"Arnie Tabor," Marie put in.

"Sure—that's three of 'em," Lacklander said. "Why do you ask, Lieutenant?"

"Because if we need to find men willing to fight, we'll have to approach those who have something to fight *for*," Matt explained. "These miners, the others who have done well, must be worried about shipping their gold or spending it, if it might mean getting their heads cracked, or worse. These are the men I would like to talk to. Them and any others you can think of."

"Still hope to organize some local law, do you, Lieutenant?"

"Hope?" Matt responded. "Yes, sir, I do hope to." From

41

up the street, three shots echoed and a man screamed in mortal pain. Matt went on, "I hope you people can respond to this and clean up this town before it's too late. If you can't, I'm afraid that by the time an army force could restore order, it just won't matter much at all to many of you."

Back at the hotel, Gus Olsen commented, "That Lacklander didn't like your answers very much, sir. I could tell that. What's the matter with these people, anyway? They expect that after they've let things go to hell in a handbasket, the government can step in and protect them?"

"They've got their minds on their own business, I expect," Kincaid said. "It takes something to stand up before a gunman and challenge him."

"Yes," Olsen said, nodding his head heavily, "I guess it does. But by God! To let them have the streets, to let them snatch away your right to live in peace . . . well, nobody's asking me," Gus said, sagging onto his cot.

I'd have no problem if Monument was full of Gus Olsens, Matt thought. But it wasn't. It was populated by miners who had come in to get rich and get out. The rest of it be damned. If your neighbor is shot down, just work twice as fast before they can get to you. Gold fever. Matt went to the window, looking out at the dark street where throngs of cursing, drinking men swirled.

A solution. Christopher Lacklander had scoffed at the idea, found it laughable. A solution beyond bringing in a squad of armed men, fighting a pitched battle in the streets of Monument. There had to be a way.

Or did there? Another shot was fired somewhere at the other end of town, and Matt Kincaid turned away from the window, wondering if Lacklander wasn't right after all.

four ================================

    Second Lieutenant Max Dunwoodie walked the boardwalk before the officers' quarters, pacing first in one direction, then in the other, as the moon floated high in the night sky. It was nearly 3:00 A.M., silent and still warm. He had finished his round of inspections, checked on the gate guard, and received a negative report. Now, as duty officer, he had no responsibilities but to stay awake. That was no problem on this hellish summer night.

He walked down past the grub hall and toward the enlisted barracks, seeing nothing, hearing nothing at all but a coyote far across the prairie, howling in defiance.

It was a night when Dunwoodie himself wished he could just howl, scream out his frustrations against the night. He had even found himself wishing the sniper would return and take a shot at someone, just to break the monotony.

He dwelled on that, on thoughts of winter—icy, shivering, numbing, bitter winter—Lord, it seemed preferable to this heat, which lay on a man's shoulders and shoved him down, draining the strength from him. The soldiers walked around in stunned apathy. They fought, they forgot to salute, they slept at odd times in odd places. Dunwoodie was allowed none of that. He was, after all, an officer.

Not that he was one of those class-conscious, strutting junior officers; at least he didn't think of himself in that way, and tried not to be. But he considered himself a leader, an example, and he considered that his dignity was worth preserving.

He tried. He did try to look crisp and sharp when he felt as wilted and sun-dazed as everyone else.

Lieutenant Dunwoodie stood in the shadow of the awning over Pop Evans's store and watched the moon float high. Even the moon seemed to give off heat, and Dunwoodie ran a finger around his collar.

He was jumpy and hot, and he felt utterly useless. What was he doing in this godforsaken place! A temporary assignment, they had termed it. The captain had Lieutenants Fitzgerald and Kincaid out in the field, and only Mr. Taylor to rely on. Dunwoodie, up from Laramie, wished to God that Fitzgerald or Kincaid would return, and quickly.

Not that Conway wasn't a good man to work for, or that he had had any particular trouble with the NCOs or enlisted men, but when he left Number Nine, Dunwoodie was not returning to Fort Laramie. He was being assigned to the small garrison at Cheyenne. And there—and there Sheila awaited him.

Sheila. He had met her at a post dance at Laramie, and for months he had tried every angle he could think of to work a transfer to the Cheyenne garrison. Finally he had

done so, and within days of his leaving he'd been temporarily assigned to Number Nine.

Temporarily! It seemed as if he had spent his entire career
at this crackerbox on the plains. Meanwhile, Sheila, by her
letters, seemed to doubt him. *"You wrote that you would
certainly be coming to the Cheyenne garrison, dear Max,
and yet now I receive a communique by post that you are
even farther away!"* she had written. *"How can I help
wondering? Didn't you inform the army of our plans?"*

Dunwoodie had to smile wryly at the recollection. Sheila
was dead serious, of course. She couldn't believe the army
would stand in the way of true love. And so she had her
doubts. Dunwoodie sighed, moved off down the moon-
shadowed boardwalk, and abruptly stopped.

That sound—his head swiveled toward the gate. There
was Private Trueblood standing watch. Nothing else moved
across the parade, in the paddock, or in the barracks. What
was that sound?

Low, snarling, primitive. He peered into the shadows.
He listened intently. A low, flapping noise. A murmur, an
echoic sound like pebbles being dropped down a pipe, rat-
tling away.

Maybe Trueblood knew what it was. He turned and
walked back to the gate. Upon reaching it, he realized that
Trueblood could not possibly know what the sound was.
He couldn't hear it, although it was Private Trueblood who
was making it.

The man was leaning against the wall, nearly at rigid
attention, snoring his damned head off. He trumpeted and
moaned, rattled, coughed, and groaned.

Dunwoodie almost wished he hadn't found him; he didn't
enjoy chewing on the men. Yet soldiers had been killed
because of sleeping guards, and there was no excuse at all
for it.

"Trueblood!"

Trueblood snapped out of it instantly. His rifle came up automatically and he jabbed it at Dunwoodie, who had to slap the muzzle away.

"Sir!" Trueblood shouted loudly.

"Private Trueblood, you were asleep on watch."

"No, sir," Trueblood blinked. For a moment he actually believed he had not been asleep. He never fell asleep on guard duty. Never! But the disorientation he felt, the officer standing before him, appearing out of nowhere, caused him to realize that he must have been asleep.

"I haven't been able to sleep for days, sir," Trueblood said anxiously. It was a serious offense, and he had been caught cold. "The heat and all. I don't know how I—"

Max Dunwoodie cut him off. He began to crawl all over Trueblood, up one side and down the other, blistering his ears, setting Trueblood's flesh crawling.

"I ought to put you on report, Trueblood."

"Yes, sir."

Dunwoodie waited a minute, a long, painful minute. "But I won't. Not this time."

Trueblood relaxed visibly, the tension draining slowly away. "Sir, I can't thank you enough."

"You can thank me. Thank me by staying awake. You've got a week of sentry duty to pull. Pull it awake. Wide, alertly awake."

"Yes, sir. I will, sir."

Dunwoodie nodded slowly and turned away. He didn't like chewing on people, never had. Trueblood had done something that was unforgiveable. Unforgiveable but inevitable at times. A man who is tired and bored is going to fall asleep. It happens. But by God, it wouldn't happen while Max Dunwoodie was duty officer.

He walked off across the parade, thinking of Sheila,

wondering when Fitzgerald would be back, when Kincaid would finish up whatever business he had at that gold town—what was the name of it, Monument?

Dunwoodie himself was getting post fever; he had to get away from Number Nine for a time, even for a few hours. There was a town over east, he had passed through it on the way over from Laramie. Another sin hole, nothing but cheap whiskey, rigged card games, and sour, used-up women. At least it would be a change. He would talk to the captain. There had to be something to do in that town!

Morning was bright, clear, and already stifling. It would be another scorcher. These hot days continued in an endless chain, breathless, enervating, numbing.

It was six in the morning when Matt Kincaid, Gus Olsen, and Private Aaron Shy went out into the main street of Monument. It was silent, eerie. The saloon doors stood wide, and a man in a white apron was sweeping the boardwalk in front of the Diamond Glen. Outside of that, there was no movement anywhere.

They passed a man lying in the street next to the boardwalk, and Olsen had to roll him over before they could determine whether he was dead or alive. He was still among the living. He moaned something and rolled away, his face plastered with mud and horse dung, his clothes stinking and stained.

There was no one at all in the restaurant when they entered, and they sat down to a breakfast of beef, beans, and cornbread.

"They serve this every meal," Gus observed wonderingly, and the waitress happened to overhear him.

"By God, you're a man who's never satisfied, aren't you?" she spat. "Gripe about supper, gripe about breakfast—Lord, you remind me of my late husband."

She stalked away and Kincaid grinned at his NCO. Gus could only shrug. "Did it again, did I?"

"Seems like it," Matt answered.

Shy set into eating with some ambition, but he paused to remark, "When I get out of this army, I'm going to live someplace where they've got chickens and know what they're for. I am going to have eggs every single morning for the rest of my natural life."

"A smart rancher would run a herd of 'em up from Texas," Gus said dryly.

"That's bad business," Kincaid said. "They're hard to handle. Nothing's worse than a chicken stampede."

"What's the plan for the day, sir?" Gus asked around a mouthful of cornbread.

"Talk to some of the miners up in the hills, I suppose, Sergeant. See if we can't set up a meeting somewhere and get these boys interested in maintaining law and order."

"Do we know him?" Shy asked. He was hunched over his plate, eating, and when Kincaid looked at him in puzzlement, Shy lifted his chin toward the door, where stood a tall man in a pearl-gray suit, a neat, wide-brimmed white hat, and shiny boots, sided by four rough-looking thugs.

"No. I don't think I want to," Kincaid admitted.

But it looked as if they were going to. The man, who moved with a rolling strut, walked to the soldiers' table and stood there silently.

"Something you want?" Kincaid asked, glancing up, dabbing his mouth with his napkin.

"I'm Frank Toomey," the tall man said, "and I want you out of my town."

Matt smiled slowly. "Sorry," he said, putting his napkin aside. "It's not your town and I'm not one of your hired morons."

One of the thugs jumped forward at that, but Toomey

48

put a hand on the gunman's shoulder.

"You don't understand, Lieutenant," Toomey said. "I don't want you hanging around, making trouble. We've got a nice little town here, and we like it the way it is."

"Sorry," Matt repeated, leaning back, "there are those who don't like the way your nice little town is. The army happens to represent those people."

"Who? Who called you in?"

"An anonymous party," Kincaid said coolly. Olsen had shifted in his chair, Matt noticed, and his hand now rested near the butt of his Scoff.

"It was Lacklander, the way I hear it," Toomey said. He leaned across the table now. His was a sharp, inhospitable face. His character was reflected perfectly in his squared chin, hollow cheeks, and sharp, nearly straight nose, but mostly in those dark, glittering eyes. They were the eyes of a man who did not know what compassion was, a man who respected no rights but his own.

"I'm glad we've had this little talk, Toomey." Kincaid rose. "But now it's over."

"It's not over. You're still here." Toomey's hand swept back his coat flap, and Matt saw the ivory-handled pistol there.

"I'm not going to shoot it out with you, Toomey. We have no quarrel. I'm not here to do you any harm."

"You lock up this town and you're harming me."

Kincaid could feel the anger mounting. His jaw clenched and his lips compressed into a straight line. Still, he fought to restrain himself. He was not paid to get into shootouts with badmen, and he had no intention of letting himself be egged into it.

But Toomey took a step too far. He reached across the table, his eyes glazed with dark glee, and grabbed Kincaid's neckerchief.

49

"Look here, soldier—"

It was as far as he got. Kincaid's right arm shot up, slapping the hand away, and his left crossed over, catching Toomey on the point of his chin. The man went down to his knees, cursing and sputtering.

One of the gunhands behind Toomey started to go for his Colt, but the click of Gus Olsen's Scoff being cocked sounded loud in the room. The gunman's hand froze in an awkward position and he shrugged, carefully raising his arms.

"Shoot him!" Toomey bellowed. He was on his knees still, blood flowing from his nose, his face crimson with anger.

"Get out of here, Toomey," Matt said coldly. "If you've got any sense you'll stay out of my path. Do you know what the penalty is for obstructing an officer of the United States Army?"

"I don't give a damn what it is," Toomey said, snatching up his hat. He got to his feet, trying to slow the flow of blood from his nose with a yellow silk scarf. "You can't get away with this. No one touches me! No one!" He was panting as he backed away, still pointing at Kincaid.

Abruptly he turned and was gone. It was a moment before Olsen holstered his pistol. Aaron Shy was a little green around the gills. Kincaid himself didn't feel rock-steady.

"That one—he'll be back, sir," Gus said. "I know his kind."

"I don't think he'll be back," Kincaid answered. "He just wanted to see how far he could push. He found out."

Olsen shook his head. He had seen men like Toomey before, and although he wouldn't have wanted Matt to stand there and take it, he knew the lieutenant had done the worst thing possible—he'd shown Toomey up in front of his men. No, Toomey wouldn't let it go.

Kincaid slid two silver dollars onto the table and picked his hat up from the bench beside him. "Let's talk to some people, Gus."

The town was starting to wake up as they emerged onto the main street. Apparently the word about the scuffle with Toomey had already gotten around town. There were a few sidelong glances at the men in blue uniforms, some whispered comments, and once a loud, mocking laugh.

Their horses were at the hastily and cheaply constructed stable at the end of the street. The hostler insisted on being paid if they were going to ride out, even though Kincaid explained patiently that they would return.

"Well," the stableman said, "that's all well and good, but you know there's ever' day a man who rides out meanin' to come back—I'm not sayin' they don't aim to—but somehow or 'nother they don't seem to make it. So that's policy—pay when you take 'em out."

Matt did so, with a shake of his head. The hostler shoved the coins into his pocket and got back to forking hay as the soldiers saddled up.

It was dry and hot outside. The town had come to life again, and it was roaring drunk, noisy, and destructive.

"Must be a different bunch of folks," Shy said as they rode out of Monument. "I can't see how anyone who survived last night would want to come back for more of the same."

They rode into the green and golden hills, grateful for the silence that settled around them as they left Monument behind. Stacks of stone—claim markers—were everywhere, although most of the claims were not being worked just now. Many of them would be sold before a shovel had so much as turned over a spadeful of earth, sold to speculators back East. Others were just-in-case claims. Just in case they started hitting ore all around the hillside.

Farther up into the hills, toward the Danby itself, there was a flurry of activity. Men crawled like ants across the slopes. The creek itself was black with panning miners. Rough shacks had been thrown up everywhere.

"Hard to believe," Shy said as they sat atop a rise, the sun burning the backs of their hands, scorching their necks. "All these folks! Kind of hurts a man's feelings to think of all of them gettin' stinkin' rich while I'm pullin' thirteen dollars a month."

"I don't see no castles," Gus Olsen said, and the Swede was right. In Colorado there were men who had actually built castles, bringing them over stone by stone from Europe. So perhaps there would be castles on these hills one day. But even in the richest gold strike, not one man in a hundred got rich, and the odds were better that a man would endure heartbreak, physical suffering, and hard weather, perhaps ruining his health for life.

But as long as there was a chance, there were always men willing to follow a rainbow.

"Let's go on down," Matt suggested, and they rode into the bottom. The miners scarcely looked up from their work. Asking directions of one of the panners, Kincaid was directed upstream to the Lacklander claim. It turned out to be a small cradling operation on a small stream feeding into the creek. Lacklander was working the cradle back and forth, alert for the first indications of color. Marie sat on a rock nearby, a Winchester across her lap. The miner seemed upset by the arrival of the soldiers.

"What is it?" Lacklander asked as he gestured to Marie, who put down her rifle and came down from the rock to work the cradle while her father talked with the soldiers. He stomped toward Kincaid in his india-rubber hip boots, mopping his sweaty forehead with a bandanna as he approached.

"I thought we'd come out and talk to you people about law and order," Kincaid said with a smile.

"Now?" Lacklander seemed genuinely flustered. It was clear that work came first. Why wouldn't it? Each moment might bring fabulous wealth.

Kincaid told him, "I'd like to talk to some of the men you mentioned. If we could set up a meeting somewhere later on and see what kind of support we have, that's the way to go. Let everyone who has an interest in maintaining order voice his opinion."

"Why can't the army simply come in?" Lacklander asked as he wiped a harried hand across his thinning gray hair. "That's the trouble, you see—we don't have time to patrol the streets and claims. If the army—"

"The army is a last resort, sir," Kincaid said more sharply than he intended.

"Yes, yes." Lacklander waved a hand and sighed. "If you can get the others to attend a meeting, I'll come as well. But just now I'm busy, as you can see."

"If you could take the time to introduce me to the others . . ."

"I am busy, Lieutenant!"

"Then perhaps," Kincaid suggested, "your daughter would be so kind."

"Marie?" Lacklander pondered and then shook his head. "I need her to stand guard."

"I would be happy to leave Sergeant Olsen and Private Shy with you," Matt suggested smoothly, and Olsen had to suppress a grin. Of all the possible solutions, Kincaid had unfalteringly gone to the best.

"Well . . . I don't care, if she doesn't," Lacklander said, looking at the two enlisted men. "I guess they'll protect my claim as well as she can."

Marie looked up from her work and her eyes, those pale,

53

pale blue eyes, were sparkling. "I don't mind, Daddy," she said. "It is important that we get things organized, after all."

"Yes, yes," Lacklander muttered. "Go ahead, then."

"There shouldn't be any problems, Sergeant," Kincaid said briskly. His eyes were on Marie, who was now tightening the cinch to her little paint pony. "Just stand by."

"Yes, sir," Olsen said, still fighting to hold back that grin. "We'll do our best."

"I'm sure you will," Kincaid said. He walked to the paint, holding the bridle while the girl, who wore jeans and a man's plaid shirt, swung up. Then he handed her the reins. "This is kind of you, Miss Lacklander," Kincaid said.

"Marie, please call me Marie." She smiled and Olsen had to turn away. That grin just couldn't be hidden any longer.

Marie led the way up a narrow draw and to the ridge above, where the dry wind was gusting. Kincaid was content to watch her silently, to watch the shifting highlights the sun formed in her dark hair. He liked the straight line of her back, her narrow waist and flaring hips. He liked the set of her shoulders, the line of her profile.

She waited atop the rise, and when he rode to join her, she said nothing. She simply sat her paint, watching back for a long minute. Then she blinked, seemed to come awake again, and said, "Arnie Tabor's claim is over the ridge. Watch yourself when we go down. He's gotten a little nervous, and he carries a big old Spencer rifle."

"All right," Matt answered softly, realizing that his eyes were on hers, that he was finding it difficult to be businesslike. "Let's go on down."

"Yes." She laughed and started her pony downslope at a walk. Soon Matt could see a rough shack, half hidden in the surrounding willows, and a squared-off excavation, timbered with unpeeled logs. A feeder creek gurgled among the willows.

"Hold it right there," a voice boomed out. Its owner remained hidden in the deep brush.

"It's Marie Lacklander, Mr. Tabor. The man with me is Lieutenant Matt Kincaid, U.S. Army."

"Army! Come a little closer."

They did so, and after a minute a long-legged, lantern-jawed man crept from the brush, holding a big .56 Spencer in his gnarled hands. He was squinting at Matt, his head cocked to one side as if that would help him to see better.

"Army?" Tabor asked, although he could certainly see the uniform. "What're you here for? Goin' to string up Frank Toomey?"

"I'm afraid I'm not prepared to go that far," Matt said, although it struck him that it might not be a bad idea. "I'd like to step down and talk to you, Mr. Tabor, if it's all right." That Spencer was still cocked, the muzzle toward Matt, and he didn't like it a bit. That was enough rifle to blow a leg clear off a man.

"Talk about what?" Arnie Tabor asked, squinting more tightly yet.

"Lieutenant Kincaid wants to talk about the trouble in Monument, Mr. Tabor. About Frank Toomey, Murray Hill, and the rest of them," Marie said.

"*Talk* about 'em. What's there to talk about? String 'em up, I say." Tabor lowered his rifle, easing the hammer down. "Get down if you've a mind to. Talk to me while I'm working. I can't set and gab all day."

Matt and Marie glanced at each other and smiled. Tabor was already stalking back through the willow brush toward his claim. Matt swung down and tied his horse to the brush, then he followed Marie through the willows. They found

Tabor working on a sluice box he was constructing. He was having trouble with the gate, apparently. Matt watched as he yanked at it and then kicked it into position.

"These other boys, they ain't got a handle on this, Kincaid. They act like this is a game out here. Going to pick up some egg-sized nuggets and get rich!" Tabor brayed a laugh. "Fools. Can't do enough with a pan to make it worth doin'. Me and Marie's pa, we're goin' about her scientific!" Tabor gave the sluice gate another kick, muttered as he knocked his ankle, and turned, wiping his muddy hands on his twill pants. "Now then, Lieutenant Kincaid, what are we talkin' about?"

"We're talking about Monument and its problems. How to make it a place where a man has a chance of surviving long enough to enjoy spending some of his gold. I want to set up a meeting with you, Lacklander, and the other miners to see if we can't thresh out some ideas on how to maintain law in these hills."

"I see," Tabor drawled. "You want us to do the army's work for you."

"It's not that, Tabor, and you should know better. Properly speaking, this is not an army job. It's the responsibility of you people, or should be."

"I ain't got time to fight Toomey and his hardcases," Tabor snorted.

"Maybe not. But tell me, how are you going to keep hold of your dust? How are you going to ship it, or get out of this territory alive, if you try to take it with you?" Matt removed his hat. "Tell me, Mr. Tabor, what are you doing with your dust now? Hiding it all in some hole in the ground?"

"None of your damn business!" Tabor said. "Beg pardon, Miss Lacklander," he added, glancing at Marie, who was perched on the sluice box watching them.

"You're better off by far banding together," Matt went on. "Send your gold out together. Stand up in front of Toomey and let him know you won't take any more."

"That's easy to say," Tabor said.

"Yes, I know that. You're right. But if something isn't done, you don't have a chance of keeping what you've worked for, and not a lot of chance of staying alive."

"Mebbe not," Tabor said thoughtfully. "Mebbe not. Well, where and when's this meeting?"

"As soon as possible. I'd like to hold it tonight. As for where, maybe you two can help me out there. Is there a building, a house?"

"I'd prefer to have it outside, myself," Tabor said. "Four walls make me feel kinda trapped. Maybe the oak grove," he suggested, looking at Marie.

"That might be best," Marie agreed. Matt was watching her, and she explained, "There's a grove of trees on top of a knoll across the Belle Fourche. You can see for miles."

"All right," Matt agreed. "It doesn't matter to me where we meet, just as long as we do." They walked back to the horses. Stepping into the saddle, Matt told Tabor, "If there's anyone you know and trust—men who are interested in protecting their lives and their property and have the backbone to do something about it, get the word to them."

Tabor agreed dourly, muttering something about Stubbs, even if he was likely a claim-jumper, and Murchison.

"Friendly cuss," Matt said as he rode up the creek with Marie. The day was horribly hot in the draw.

"Well, they've all gotten that way. Jittery is what they are, like my father. I'm the same way," she said with a nervous laugh. "I can't sleep nights. We can hear shots from town, and sometimes nearer. There's mornings we find a man dead in the river." She shrugged. "It's happened so much, it's not even news any longer."

57

They passed several empty camps littered with tin cans and scraps of wood, and finally rounded the bend in the creek, finding a horde of men at the point where the feeder creek ran into the Danby itself.

Here, high bluffs rose above the sparkling water. A shanty town had grown up along one bank. "That's Clive Scales's claim," Marie said, pointing. "He's got the first claim—and the richest, they say. He was one of the men who found the—" Her voice suddenly broke off, and Matt looked at her in puzzlement.

"He found what?" Kincaid asked.

"His claim," she said nonsensically, and Matt could see he was going to get nowhere by pressing it.

Clive Scales was more tight-lipped and, if possible, more bristly than Arnie Tabor. He wanted nothing to do with Toomey, the army, Kincaid. All he wanted was to work his claim.

"And then do what with the gold, sir?" Matt asked. Again he wondered how these men were planning to get their dust out of here, what they were doing with it in the meantime. Scales's claim was large, and they said it was prime, but he had done little to improve it. He had simply marked off a section of the creek with wire stretched from bank to bank.

"That's mine and everybody knows it," he said, tugging at his full gray beard. "They also know that anybody who sets foot on it without my invite will get himself shot—that's *my* law and order."

"That sort of law and order hasn't been working too well up here, has it?" Matt asked. Scales, he noticed, had never answered the question about where he was keeping his gold. These men were a close-mouthed bunch, jealous of their claims, wary of everyone.

"We're going to have a meeting this evening at the oak grove, do you know where that is?"

"'Course I do," Scales growled. "But I don't know what good a meetin's goin' to do." Nevertheless, he agreed to come and bring along several of the others.

Kincaid and Marie had to ride a mile upstream to find George Bestwick's claim. Bestwick was young and vigorous. His shoulders were burned red by the sun. He stood panning in an oxbow formed by the stream; a pistol was shoved into the top of his waders.

"Any luck?" Kincaid shouted, and Bestwick's hand dropped automatically to his weapon.

"Who wants to know?"

"Mind if we come over? I'll tell you."

"Come on ahead," Bestwick said, recognizing Marie Lacklander. Still, he watched their approach warily, his eyes going to the opposite bank, searching the willows.

Bestwick was no more eager to take an active part in keeping the law than any of the others had been. He agreed to the meeting, however. Bestwick had led them to a fallen log where he sat, wiped his sunburned forehead with his wrist, and listened to Kincaid's often-repeated speech.

Matt had had occasion to glance down at the pan Bestwick had brought from the river, and although he was no miner, he could see no trace of gold dust, even in a minute quantity, in that pan. Of course, every pan wouldn't be laden with color, but it seemed odd. Bestwick's claim was supposed to be one of the richest.

There were many explanations—perhaps the man was trying a new area. But then, if there was dust in the river, it should occur everywhere in trace quantities. Bestwick had his eyes on Kincaid.

Seeing that, Matt stood quickly and said, "Think it over in the meantime, and we'll see you at the meeting tonight. Bring any trustworthy men you can think of."

"Yeah." Bestwick was suddenly cagey. He stood and

shifted his body between Kincaid and the pan. "So long, Miss Lacklander."

"Goodbye, Mr. Bestwick."

They mounted silently and rode northward a little ways through the heat of the day. The sun glittered off the river, blinding them. The sounds of working fell away and Matt, aware of it, asked, "Whose claim is up this way?"

"Why, no one's," Marie said with a brilliant smile. "No one's at all." She smiled again and Matt straightened in the saddle. He followed her deeper into the willows.

five ⸻⸻⸻⸻⸻⸻

Matt Kincaid followed silently as Marie Lacklander rode her small paint pony up through the willow glen and onto a grassy knoll studded with scattered manzanita and sage. A single, wind-battered cedar stood on a bench at the northern end of the knoll.

Riding to the cedar, Marie stepped down and Matt followed suit.

They had a lovely view of the valley, the Belle Fourche running past appearing as a broad silver-blue ribbon. They could see no sign of Monument, no manmade scars. They could not hear the picks falling, the mules braying, the muttered curses of the miners.

There was only the wind sound, the song of a jay deep in the manzanita brush.

Marie walked to Matt and stood before him speculatively. Her pale blue eyes were bright, her mouth turned up in a half-smile.

Matt didn't need invitations. His arms went around her waist and he drew her to him, kissing her mouth, which was warm, moist, eager.

She pulled away, letting her hand trail down his shoulder and chest. Walking into the dry shade of the cedar, she slowly unbuttoned her shirt. Matt heard a humming sound—cicadas, he thought at first, but it was the blood racing in his ears.

Her shirt fell open and two full, round breasts bobbed free. Matt swallowed hard, and Marie smiled. She threw her shirt aside and stretched out her arms. Matt walked to her, held her tightly for a minute, and then felt her small hands push him away.

Her fingers worked down the front of his shirt. She tugged his shirttails up out of his waistband and pressed herself against him. Her breasts were warm and soft against his hard-muscled chest.

"I thought it would be nice to have a little picnic before we went back, Matt," Marie said teasingly. "Do you like picnics?"

"Most times. But we haven't brought anything to eat."

"That's the least important part," she said. She kissed him again, her lips taking Kincaid's lower lip. Her tongue ran across his teeth, and she abruptly pulled away again.

"That's the appetizer," she said, and Matt noticed that her voice was a little husky. Now she kicked off her boots, and sitting on her shirt, she pulled off her pants.

Matt's pulse started to race violently in his temples. Her legs were short, but perfect. There wasn't an ounce of fat on her thighs. Her calves tapered perfectly to her ankles.

Marie sat on her shirt, biting at her lower lip. Her fingers wriggled in a gesture of urgency and Matt went to her, sinking to his knees beside her. Immediately her fingers went to the fly of his trousers and Matt felt the warm touch of her hands, heard the murmured sounds from deep in Marie's throat as she fondled him, her eyes half shut, her head lolling on her neck as if its weight were too much for her.

"Matt—here, please!" She turned and got to hands and knees. Then her head lowered to rest on her folded forearms and Matt was left with the astonishing, absolutely compelling view of her upthrust white buttocks. Full, smooth, white, and magnetic.

"Please, Matt," she said quietly, and she didn't have to beg. He eased up behind her as she slowly spread her legs. On his knees, Matt ran his hands across the pale half-globes of her buttocks, lowering his lips to kiss the silky flesh there, his nostrils filling with the musky woman-scent of Marie Lacklander.

She had spread herself now, and Matt's thumbs found her cleft, gently exploring, invading, stroking her dewy inner flesh.

"Please!" she said in a cracked exhortation, and he moved nearer to her, his pelvis contacting the soft, pale flesh of Marie's ass. Her hand reached between her legs and groped for his erection. Finding it, she positioned him, rocking slowly backward and forward until he inched into her, sensation flooding him.

His loins began to throb dully, and the perspiration glistened on his flesh as the dry heat of the day, added to the heat of the inner furnaces, raised his temperature intolerably.

Marie had her face buried against her arms. She was faceless, voiceless temporarily. Her essence was contained in those broad, muscular hips. A terrible machine of amazing power, of ravenous needs.

63

Matt moved forward, burying himself in the woman. They remained motionless for long moments, but only externally. Within their bodies they were pulsing, readjusting, trickling, demanding.

Matt could take no more of that motionlessness, and he began to sway against her, bringing a satisfied, deeply pleasured sound from Marie's throat. She turned her head now, and Matt could see that her eyes were glazed; her mouth set with intense concentration. He rested his hands on her upthrust hips and continued to rock against her.

The day grew warmer. Liquid fire seemed to flow through Matt's veins. His head was filled still with a whirring as of many insects. His thighs trembled and as he saw Marie go rigid, lift her head, and with tense concentration hold her breath, he reached a sudden powerful climax.

He sagged against her, grasping for her breasts. She went flat on her belly and then rolled to him, and they lay together, their perspiration-glossed bodies warm as they pressed together. The sunlight through the cedar branches mottled her body. Her eyes glittered from out of the shifting shadows and he held her tightly, feeling at one with the raw land, with this woman.

It was nearly sunset before they returned to the Lacklander claim, but if Christopher Lacklander noticed it, he said nothing. He still worked intently, his eyes fixed on the cradle.

Matt swung down with only a single intense glance at Marie, who met his gaze and turned her head quickly. Then he walked to where Gus Olsen sat propped up against the fallen tree trunk, watching the river and the feverishly working men. Aaron Shy started to come to his feet, but Matt waved him back down.

"Any luck, sir?" Gus asked with a hint of innuendo.

"Some, I think," Matt answered, giving nothing away.

He told Olsen about the meeting that evening at the oak knoll.

"Well, that's a start," Olsen said, barely stifling a yawn.

Lacklander was talking in a low voice to his daughter. As the three soldiers watched, he straightened up and stood, hands on hips, stretching his back.

"He find any color?" Matt asked.

"No, sir," Olsen responded, "he didn't. Says he's got a rich claim, but I'm damned if I see how he figures."

"Tell you somethin'," Private Shy put in, "it's as rich as any on this stretch of creek."

Kincaid looked at him. "What do you mean, Shy?"

"Well, sir," Shy said as he rose stiffly and planted his hat, "there wasn't a whole lot to do while we were standing watch, and so I kind of wandered around, up and down the creek, you see."

"Yes?" Matt prompted him impatiently.

"Well, what I mean, sir—Mr. Lacklander's having the same kind of luck as everyone else. I didn't see a fleck of gold dust nowhere. These boys don't want to talk about what they're doing, of course, but they didn't have to say much. I didn't see nobody—and that is not a single, solitary soul—tuck no gold dust away."

"Well," Olsen shrugged, "these men have got the wrong fork of the creek, I reckon. They gambled and lost. Everyone can't strike it."

Kincaid's eyes narrowed. Sundown was painting the sky orange and deep purple. Lacklander had had no luck. A bad stretch of the river, maybe, but he wondered. The idea was so unlikely that he was tempted to discard it immediately, but he couldn't quite release it.

He had seen *no* gold. Not a trace of it on either fork of the creek. Of course, those who had it were likely hiding it. Still . . . he thought of Bestwick, who was near where the best claims were said to be. He had not shown color either.

There had to be gold, didn't there? These hundreds of men didn't all converge upon Monument for no reason. No, someone had gold, but Matt wondered . . . how many of them would find nothing at all?

"Something wrong, sir?" Olsen asked, noticing the abstracted gaze in Kincaid's eyes.

"I don't know, Sergeant. I honestly don't know." He looked again to the skies. "Let's get going. We'll be late for the meeting."

It was nearly dark, still blazing hot. The sun wouldn't loosen its grip. Long violet fingers of light stained the sky. Private Trueblood relieved Armstrong and went out to make his perimeter check.

He moved through the twilight of the plains like a shadow. A heavy-eyed shadow. Trueblood hadn't slept for nights—it seemed like weeks, although everyone told him it wasn't possible.

There had been one nap, that one short nap—on guard duty, and he had to get caught by Mr. Dunwoodie. *Guard duty stinks,* Trueblood muttered to himself. Three hours on, three off. Supposedly to keep the guards alert. It seemed to work just the opposite. You couldn't sleep, and if you did, what was three hours of sleep anyway? Trueblood wondered idly if he could somehow wangle a pass, although no one had been having much luck. Cohen was as grouchy as a February bear.

Once he had fallen asleep in the barracks. Once! And then that damned fight had erupted between Bill Fox and Amos Brandt. Those two were going crazy in harness. Fox had set him up with that pail of water, and Brandt was still crazy mad over it.

But Fox was the one people were worried about—he

was starting to giggle a lot, to dance around crazily. If there was someone who was really going to snap, it was Fox.

Trueblood passed the point where the shot had been taken at Hollis, and let out a sigh of relief. He never passed there without feeling his muscles tighten a little, his stomach knot up. But that Cheyenne was long gone by now, he supposed.

He swung around the corner, peering out at the twilight-shrouded plains. That light could play tricks on you, making you doubt your own vision. Trueblood kept his eyes close to the stockade, searching for...what? A Cheyenne lying close by, a band of thieves waiting to overrun the outpost? He had never yet seen anything or anybody, but regulations were—

The shot boomed out of the twilight, its rolling echo thundering across the plains. Trueblood felt his arm jerked away from his body, felt himself spun around, and he threw himself to the earth, his heart pounding madly.

He brought his Springfield around automatically, but there was nothing to shoot at. Nothing but the shadowed plains, empty and ominous. He braced himself, waiting for a second shot, but there was none.

Slowly, then, the trembling set in. Trueblood's legs twitched and his teeth clattered. He heard footsteps behind him and spun around, lifting the muzzle of his rifle before he saw the uniforms.

McBride was in the lead, and on his heels was Lieutenant Dunwoodie. Five or six other men were just rounding the corner of the stockade.

"What happened?" Dunwoodie asked, showing his intelligence by immediately flattening himself out.

"Sniper," Trueblood said, his throat oddly constricted.

"Did he get you?"

"I don't know!" Trueblood laughed. "I thought he did, but I don't feel nothing."

"Where?"

"The arm," Trueblood said, and McBride poked at his sleeve. Reb whistled.

"Look at that!"

Dunwoodie's head swiveled that way, and in the darkness he could see McBride's finger protruding from Trueblood's coat sleeve.

"Right on through. Couldn't have missed by half an inch."

"You didn't see anything?" Dunwoodie asked again, his face anxious.

"No, sir, not a damned thing." Trueblood had made no move to rise. He wasn't anxious to see if that marksman could do better.

"The same as with Hollis," the officer muttered.

"Could you tell what he was using?" Reb thought to ask.

"I'm not sure. It had kind of a flat report, you know. Likely a Sharps, I think. Not the big .50, but a carbine, .45-70, or maybe .45-90. Just a guess, but one of Windy's Delawares, Joseph Hatchet, used to carry a little Sharps."

"How far out was he, Trueblood?" Dunwoodie wanted to know.

"Oh, he was out there, sir. I never saw smoke—that alone makes me think he was at least three hundred yards. The sound came rollin' a long ways after the bullet hit."

It was dark and silent now, and Dunwoodie said, "Let's get inside, make sure you're not hit."

And report to Captain Conway; he was going to hit the ceiling. Trueblood got to his feet, finding his knees a little rubbery. He wobbled against Reb, smiled sheepishly, and was turned and escorted into Number Nine.

Captain Conway hit the ceiling.

He was on his way across the parade, pistol in hand, when he saw Trueblood being steered into the barracks and

68

Malone, as replacement guard, heading for the gate.

Entering the barracks, he found Trueblood, shirt stripped off, sitting at a table. Dunwoodie hovered over him, and Reb McBride, spotting Conway, started to call the barracks to attention before the captain waved him off irritably.

"Hit?" Conway asked first.

Dunwoodie spun around in surprise, "No, sir, but damn near."

He showed Conway the coat Trueblood had been wearing. Conway shoved a finger through the bullet hole, then he breathed a slow curse and tossed the coat aside.

"And you saw nothing this time either?" Conway wanted to know.

"Nothing, sir," Trueblood answered. He repeated his story, saying again that all he knew was that the man was likely using a Sharps carbine.

Lieutenant Taylor had put in an appearance soon enough to hear the last of Trueblood's story, and he stood in the doorway of the enlisted barracks, watching the anger and tension on the faces of officers and men.

Again, Conway was impatient to do something about this situation, but again there was little that could be done. It was fully dark outside now, and whoever it had been was presumably long gone.

Conway led the way back to his own quarters, Taylor and Dunwoodie trailing after him. Flora was waiting anxiously, peering from the door.

"Let's go inside and have a drink, gentlemen," Conway suggested. Dunwoodie, as duty officer, was technically on duty, but he had no objections if the captain didn't.

"Was anyone hurt?" Flora asked.

"No. It was Private Trueblood. He was sniped at, had part of his sleeve ripped away. It was, however," Conway said, "very close."

"And how close will it be next time?" Taylor said. He accepted a glass of bourbon from Warner Conway.

The captain's face was grim. "There won't be a next time. I won't have it."

Conway paced the floor for a minute. Flora sat, hands folded in her lap, watching him. He stopped, drank his whiskey, and turned to Taylor.

"I want you out there at first light tomorrow, Mr. Taylor. I want that ground searched inch by inch. We're not dealing with a phantom here. He must be leaving some sort of sign, damn it! Who's your tracker?"

"Malone, sir," Taylor said almost apologetically.

"He didn't find anything last time, did he?"

"No, sir. But he's still our best, for my money. He's done some decent work in the past." Taylor took a swallow of liquor. "If only Windy were around."

"Well, he's not. He's taking those sodbusters through the South Pass." Conway sat in his chair, his expression sour. Flora shot a sympathetic glance at Mr. Taylor.

"I won't have my men shot at," Conway said gravely. "I want this halted, *now*. Any suggestions?"

Dunwoodie could only shake his head. Taylor had one thought.

"Maybe we ought to see what we can find out from the local friendlies, sir," the junior officer suggested. "Interview the Indians down in Tipi Town. It still seems likely that we've got a renegade potshooting us. Maybe someone down there has heard whisperings."

"That's worth a try," Conway agreed. "Unfortunately, it's another job that Windy would be perfect for. He speaks the lingo."

"Wojensky can speak it some," Taylor said by way of recommendation.

"Yes, all right. Mr. Dunwoodie—I'll leave that to you.

70

Take Corporal Wojensky with you in the morning, get down across the deadline, and see if the Cheyenne know anything about this sniper. Taylor, take Malone and comb that area out there. And I do mean comb it!"

"Yes, sir." Taylor rose with a sigh. "Any word from Fitz or Kincaid, sir?"

"Nothing yet. Fitzgerald has no way of sending word. I frankly don't expect to hear from him until he rides through the gate. And I don't know when that will be. Those renegades are still raising hell, according to a buffalo hunter who passed through yesterday. As for Matt—I hope I *don't* hear from him. If I do, it will be a request for a squad of soldiers. I wonder if that town's as wild as the reports had it." Conway was meditative. "Well, that's it, gentlemen. If you come up with any new angles on this, please don't hesitate to suggest them. Once might have been a fluke. Twice scares hell out of me—it suggests a pattern. And," he added solemnly, "I am not one of those who believes the third time is always a charm. Someone is going to get killed if we don't find this sniper of ours, gentlemen. Give it some thought."

Trueblood *was* giving it a lot of thought. Yes, it was dark when he went to the gate again to relieve Malone, but who was to say the sniper wouldn't creep nearer? Who was to say the next shot wouldn't finish his career abruptly?

Trueblood was dog-tired, but he had no fears of falling asleep this night. He had those devils riding him, prodding at his brain. There was someone out there who wanted to kill him.

"What've you got, one more turn around the post?" Malone asked.

"One more, then it's Armstrong's turn, bless his little heart."

Malone smiled crookedly and then, his voice unchar-

71

acteristically mild, he said, "Good luck, True. Watch your butt, will you?"

"Don't worry about that," Trueblood muttered. The night was dark. It would be hours before the moon rose. Dark and hot. Damn this heat! Wouldn't it ever break?

He glanced at his watch, saw that he had a scant ten minutes before making his last perimeter check, and sighed. The post was unusually silent. Pop Evans's store was open, but there was no one there. From time to time, Trueblood could see a man come to the barracks door and peer out, see the faces behind him.

What the hell were they doing? Knowing these boys, they were probably betting on whether or not Trueblood would survive his watch.

Trueblood turned away and stared out at the dark, vast plains, seeing nothing, hearing nothing but the distant screech of a hunting owl. He glanced at his watch again, felt his hand trembling, and cursed himself.

"You've been in tighter spots, what's the matter with you?" he demanded angrily.

It was true. He had been in much tighter spots, but there was something intimidating about this. It was eerie, haunting. Someone was out there—someone invisible. Who he was, what he wanted, you didn't know...except that he liked to shoot at soldiers.

If he would stand up, shout, challenge—Trueblood figured that in that case it would be easy to march toward him, man to man, gun in hand. Let the best man win. But when you didn't know what you were facing, when the man was invisible, nameless, motiveless, unpredictable, it was enough to chill your guts.

He looked at his watch and actually gave a start when he realized it was time to go out. Damn them! Turning around, he saw the faces in the doorway—a fine bunch of friends. Trueblood opened the sentries' gate and went out, his spine crawling with apprehension.

He moved quickly, his gait stiff, along the wall, not taking a breath until he had rounded the first corner. Not slowing a bit, he passed the spot where Hollis had been shot at, achieved the next corner, and turned sharply in the darkness. Just up ahead there... he involuntarily hunched his shoulders and had to force himself to remain at a walk. His muscles urged him to sprint for the corner.

Trueblood was too much a soldier to give in to urges like that. Steeling himself, he marched past the spot where that bullet had tugged at his sleeve, like death tapping him on the shoulder, introducing himself, and he was by.

Turning the fourth corner, he had the gate in view and he slowed down just a hair. Then he was in, the gate locked behind him, and he closed his eyes, taking a deep slow breath.

He glanced toward the barracks, saw the faces still peering at him, and muttered, "You unholy bastards!" Then, his body gradually loosening, his heart slowing, his breathing becoming less shallow and labored, he resumed his watch. It was only an hour now before Armstrong showed up to relieve him.

Trueblood found himself suddenly relaxed. So relaxed that his legs threatened to give way. The tension was gone, and the nights of sleeplessness weighed heavily.

With a jerk he pulled himself alert. Mr. Dunwoodie had caught him sleeping on guard once. He wouldn't be able to ignore it a second time. Trueblood smiled thinly, wryly. He had missed being shot by the sniper, but falling asleep on duty again just might get him shot by the army.

The forces of the world were lined up against Trueblood on that night, it seemed. Snipers, officers, heat, and long watches.

He wouldn't sleep. He yawned as he thought that. *I won't fall asleep.* But he seemed hardly able to support his own weight. Minutes before, he had been so wound up that nothing could have induced him to close his eyes. Now, with the tension gone . . . he yawned again, mightily, so that his jaw felt that it might unhinge and tears flowed from his eyes.

Trueblood braced himself against the wall. One hour to go. He knew he could make it an hour. His eyes started to close, but he wouldn't allow it. With an effort of sheer willpower, he forced his eyes to open wide. One hour. Then Armstrong could worry about getting sniped at; Trueblood was going to sleep.

Lieutenant Dunwoodie prowled the parade, moving through the deep shadows. He was on edge. It was not only the sniper, but h_ had received another letter from Sheila. Another smooth, slightly snide letter.

"*. . . I'm sure, my darling, that you have done everything possible to expedite your reassignment to the Cheyenne garrison. I understand. Poppa and Aunt Millie, however, not to mention my friends, all of whom are dying to meet you, cannot understand why you are delaying . . .*"

Damn the woman! It would be easy to be angry with her if it weren't for vivid memories of her soft, pouting lips, her childlike, so-wise eyes. Dunwoodie was certain of one thing—he had to get the hell out of here!

Where was Fitzgerald, where was Kincaid! Damn it, there was no way in hell he could go to Conway and say, "My fiancee wants me reassigned right now, please be so good as to cut my orders."

Sheila. She was a goddess by moonlight, with her hair like spun gold, her breast heaving with emotion until he reached out to kiss her. Then she would fall away, suddenly coy, suddenly unattainable.

74

Dunwoodie felt a stirring in his loins, and he knew he had better get his mind off Sheila. Bless her soul—she was young, too young, but he would teach her. She would learn. All young women went through these uncertainties. They didn't understand the army way at all.

It gave him pause to stop and consider. Dunwoodie was army, meant to remain army. Too many of these little episodes wouldn't do at all . . . He shook it off. She was only young, yearning for him. He had to get the hell off this post!

Dunwoodie walked toward the gate, feeling itchy, hot, lonely. He saw Trueblood at attention, staring at him.

Dunwoodie waved a hand. Sure, he had caught the man sleeping, but that was no reason for Trueblood to have to come to attention like that.

Rigid attention. Maybe he had frightened the soldier. Dunwoodie frowned and waved a hand again, but Trueblood didn't relax a bit. He stood, eyes staring, at stiff attention.

I'll leave, he thought. *The man is scared to death.* And he turned, striding back toward the officers' quarters, his thoughts shifting again, inexorably, to the woman waiting for him in Cheyenne.

"See if you can do better!" Rafferty called after Armstrong. Armstrong, who was going out to relieve Trueblood, failed to see the humor in any of it.

There had been a pool on Trueblood; the bets were on how quickly Private Trueblood would make the circuit in the aftermath of the sniper's attack. It had turned out to be damned quickly. Rafferty had won the pool. Now we was doubling up on Armstrong.

"Not funny, Rafferty," Armstrong said. "A man risks his neck and you bastards want to put money on it."

Armstrong went out, feeling jumpy already. He knew they meant nothing by it; it was a way of fighting nervousness in itself. Every man in the barracks would have his turn on the gate, and there were some counting the days until their trick came up, hoping to God the sniper was caught by then.

Still . . . Armstrong walked to the gate, watching Trueblood as he approached. Damn, for a man who complained about how beat he was, Trueblood seemed alert as hell. Standing at attention, eyes wide . . . Armstrong frowned and went up to him.

"Here you go, Trueblood."

Trueblood didn't respond, and then Armstrong, looking closer, figured out why. Asleep on his feet with his eyes open!

"Well, damn me!" Armstrong murmured. He reached out hesitantly and touched Trueblood's shoulder.

"I'm not asleep," Trueblood said immediately. "I'm not asleep, Mr. Dunwoodie."

Then he turned and marched off toward the barracks. Armstrong didn't think Trueblood had ever seen him. He watched Trueblood go, shaking his head in disbelief. Then, taking a deep, slow breath, Armstrong went out to take his first circuit. He didn't glance back toward the barracks; he knew what he would see. And he made someone very happy. He must have broken Trueblood's record by at least thirty seconds.

six

The meeting at the oak grove had broken up. It hadn't gone all that well, in Matt Kincaid's opinion. The general opinion was that the army ought to move in, the army ought to get rid of Toomey, the army ought to stand by and protect the miners while they worked their claims. Matt's arguments to the contrary hadn't been heeded.

"Look," he had explained carefully, "it would be fine if we had the men to spare, but we haven't. Martial law can be imposed, but I'm not that sure you men would appreciate the terms under which that law would be administered. You're better off by far to get together, form some sort of law enforcement committee and take care of your local problems by yourselves."

"Better off!" Clive Scales was the speaker, and he was

incensed. "Better off to let our claims lay idle while we play lawman? Let's face it, Kincaid. You want us to do this job because it's best for the army. You want to get out of doing what needs to be done."

"Your people are paid to fight, aren't they?" Arnie Tabor demanded. "Well, we're not."

"We've got the same rights as some damn sodbuster out on the plains, don't we?" Bestwick asked. His face was red. A murmur of agreement went up. "You protect them from the Indians, why can't you protect us from cutthroats like Toomey? As far as that goes, why don't you just arrest him right now? Take him away and hang him."

"I can't do that, Mr. Bestwick, and you know it. Not until—and if—Monument is placed under martial law. If you people would hold yourselves an election, appoint a judge and town marshal—"

"Then you could go home!"

Matt stood looking at the faces around him. It was already dark in the oak grove, but he could read the frustration and anger in their expressions.

"Look," he said, trying another approach, "even if we do move in, you know it will be a time before more soldiers can arrive from Number Nine. Even a few days will be too much of a delay for some of you."

"Then why in hell didn't you bring more soldiers with you!" Scales wanted to know. That brought another round of grumbling.

"Let me ask you something," Kincaid went on. "What are you doing now for temporary protection? When you want to ship gold, you must have a party of armed men for guards. How are you managing that?"

Astonishingly, he was met with silence after asking that. "Mr. Scales?"

"I don't care to say," Scales muttered, plucking at his beard.

"Bestwick?"

"I don't use no guards. I haven't shipped any dust."

"You keep it hidden up here? Where someone might stumble over it?" Kincaid was incredulous.

"I don't think it's your business what I'm doing with it, Kincaid. I can't see that's it's got a damn thing to do with anything else."

"So you're doing nothing with your gold dust." Kincaid looked from one man to the next. The old oaks around them stood dark against a dark sky. "Because you're scared to move it? What happens if you do get killed? It doesn't have to be Toomey's work, either. What happens if you get snakebit, if your horse rolls on you, if you fall off the rocks and break your neck? Most of you must have family somewhere. How are they going to get along? If you men are just squirreling away your dust, I think it's a damned poor idea."

"I still don't think it's your business, Lieutenant." Clive Scales had taken it upon himself to act as spokesman. His claim was one of the first and supposedly one of the richest. The bearded miner straightened himself and said, "I think I feel like everyone else here. We've work to do. We're not gunfighters—that's why we called in the army in the first place. Nosing around, asking about our dust is getting us nowhere. The army's draggin' its feet on this. We need twenty, thirty soldiers in here, and we need 'em now. You're worried about our families? Keep us alive, that's the way to help them out."

There was a little more discussion, none of it getting them any closer to agreement. Finally, Scales announced that this foolishness was just a waste of time. He wanted the army in now, and he was going back to sit watch over his claim.

That effectively ended the meeting. Wandering off in groups of two or three, the miners, muttering together, returned to the hills, leaving Matt and his men alone on the knoll.

"Well, that's that, I reckon," Gus Olsen said. He was crouched against the earth, sketching in the dirt with a stick. "These folks aren't going to lift a finger to help themselves. We've done all we can, it looks like we're going to have to give the captain some bad news."

"I'm not so sure." Kincaid was looking off into the distance. He could see the lights from Monument through the trees. "I'm not so sure we've done all we can just yet, Sergeant."

"Then what, sir?" Shy asked. He still had dark visions of the three of them becoming a provisional police department, and he didn't like the idea at all.

"I'm not sure." Kincaid was tight-lipped, but Gus Olsen could almost see the gears whirling around in the officer's head. "This whole thing hinges on . . ." He fell silent again for a moment, then roused himself and said, "Come along, men. I want to talk to some people."

"Who? We've talked to everyone already." Shy muttered this thought; it wasn't his place to challenge an officer, but he couldn't see exactly what point there was in talking to any of the prospectors again. He hoped to God Kincaid didn't intend to talk to that Toomey character. That was an evil-looking man, and he had some tough customers siding him. That big redhead, Murray Hill—brr! Shy was greatly relieved when Kincaid sheared off and rode his horse away from town, back toward the Danby Creek claims.

Kincaid was silent as they rode. The night was warm. He felt sticky, grimy, needing a bath badly. It didn't seem that the weather was ever going to break.

They rode across the Danby by starlight, and came up on the Lacklander camp. Kincaid called out before they entered, not wanting to get shot by mistake.

Christopher Lacklander was already in his longjohns. He had a scattergun in his hands and his expression was far from friendly.

"Now what, Kincaid? God, don't you ever let go?"

"No." Matt swung down from his horse. "Lacklander, it's my job to try to straighten up this situation. I would think you people would want to see it cleaned up, but I can't tell it from the amount of cooperation I've been getting."

"All right, what do you want?" Lacklander asked with suspicion and weariness both in his voice. "I've got to get some sleep."

"Just a little more talk," Kincaid said. Marie Lacklander had appeared at her father's shoulder. She was still dressed, although she had unpinned her dark hair and it fell pleasingly across her shoulders. The low glow of the lantern, inside the shabby tent that was their home, illuminated her smile. "If you'd allow it, sir," Kincaid went on, "your daughter should be able to give me any information I need."

"Well..." Lacklander shrugged. "Long as you stay in camp." He looked at Shy and Olsen, who had also dismounted and now stood behind their lieutenant. "Go ahead, hell, go ahead!" He waved a hand and stalked into the tent.

Marie, smiling faintly, her hands behind her back, came forward.

"Can I help you, Lieutenant?" she asked with a smile and a meaning that was apparent only to Lieutenant Kincaid.

"Just a little conversation," he answered, and the smile seemed to flatten a little.

"Oh. All right."

81

She crossed to the dead fire and poked it a little, stirring the embers to life. She added a few dry sticks, and the fire blazed cheerfully.

"It's not the heat I want," she said, stating the obvious, since the night continued oppressively warm, "but it's nice to be able to see who you're speaking to."

Shy reflected that this was so. It wasn't hurting his eyes any to look at Marie Lacklander, but—just his luck—it didn't take much perception to see she had eyes only for Lieutenant Kincaid.

"I don't have many new questions to ask," Kincaid began. "But what I need, what I hope to have, are some honest answers to the old questions."

"The old questions?" Marie's eyebrows arched.

"The old questions. The hints. The suspicions. Something is not quite right in Monument, Marie."

"There's a lot that isn't right in Monument," Marie replied with a laugh.

"Yes." Matt nodded. He smiled at Marie, and taking her hand, he went on, "Let me put it to you directly. Do you realize that in the time we have spent in Monument, we have seen not a single ounce of gold from any of the claims?"

"Well, of course not," Marie said. "That's because no one wants to show it."

"Maybe." Matt held up a hand. "But do you think it's likely? I've seen men working on what are supposed to be the richest claims on the creek, seen their panning, seen nothing. Not a trace of gold. Private Shy reported the same curious situation—he saw no one with gold, no one panning any color along this entire stretch of the creek."

"I know," Marie admitted with a sigh. "There hasn't been a lot found on this fork of the Danby. As much as I hate to say it, I think my father's claim may be worthless."

82

She poked at the fire with a stick, drawing sparks. The night was warm, her eyes distracted. Firelight played on her face.

"It's the west fork where everyone has hit it," Marie said.

"Clive Scales?"

"Yes."

"And Arnie Tabor, George Bestwick?" Matt asked. The girl looked at him with some befuddlement.

"Why, yes. Everyone knows they've done well up there."

"Everyone knows." Matt gestured, palms up. "*How* does everyone know? Have you seen their gold, Marie? Has your father?"

"They're very cagey," she answered.

"And more," Matt said.

A falling star streaked across the night sky. No one but Aaron Shy seemed to notice it. He followed it with his eyes until it burst into short-lived flame and was gone, leaving the sky as dark and empty as ever.

"I don't understand," Marie Lacklander was saying. "What are you trying to prove, Matt? What has any of this to do with solving the problem of Monument? My father hasn't found gold, nor have some of the others. Their pride doesn't allow them to admit that. Others have found gold, and they're keeping their mouths shut. If it were known, Toomey and his men would move in and take it away from them—by force, I imagine."

"Then doesn't it make sense to transport the gold dust out of Monument?" Matt asked. He rose and turned to face her, his back to the low burning fire. "Wouldn't *you* do that? Move the gold to a bank in, say, Laramie or Cheyenne?"

"Why, yes," Marie said, her eyes confused, questioning. What was Matt getting at?

"No one has."

She frowned and looked away briefly before raising her eyes to stare at him.

"No one?"

"No one at all," Matt said briskly. "No one has moved any dust out of here. Not a grain."

"Or they're not admitting it," Olsen put in.

"Yes." Matt nodded. "But why not admit *that?* What could it hurt, with the gold long gone, safely banked?"

"It is odd," Marie said quietly. "But I don't quite see where this is leading us. No one has had the time or the inclination to move their gold dust to another area. Perhaps everyone is afraid of trying. Perhaps they are hiding it."

"Perhaps there is no gold," Matt said suddenly.

Marie's face was immobile. Then she laughed, pointing a finger at Matt. "You're joking."

"Joking? Why?" He moved nearer, bending over her, his eyes serious, penetrating.

"But why would they all pretend they have found gold?" She laughed again.

"I haven't heard a single man say he has!" Matt commented. "Your father says Tabor and Scales have gold. Someone says Bestwick must have a rich claim. Yet no one has said, 'Sure, I've found it, here's a sample.'"

Marie argued, "Everyone knows that there's gold. Everyone knows who has the richest claims."

"How? How in blazes do they know? I don't know," Matt said, touching his fingertips to his chest, "because I haven't seen a sign of color. I haven't seen an ounce of dust. I haven't heard of a single man shipping any gold out of Monument. None! So how, Marie, just how do they know that there is gold, that there are men panning it?"

"Well, it's—" Her voice broke off. She shrugged and then simply sat looking at Matt.

"How long have you been here, Marie?"

"Me? Six weeks."

"Have you ever seen any gold?"

"Of course," she answered, and Matt's eyes narrowed. That was not the reply he was expecting at this point. Maybe his imagination had been running away with him, after all.

"You have?"

"Certainly. Everyone saw it." She smiled. "Well, not the gold itself, actually, but I saw the coffin."

Matt shook his head in mild confusion. "The *coffin?* What in the world are you talking about, Marie?"

"The coffin. How do you think this all got started, Matt?"

She was looking at him with open, firelit eyes and Matt could only stare at her as if she were speaking a foreign language. He glanced at Sergeant Olsen, who could only shrug in response.

"The coffin?"

"Yes," Marie replied. "I thought you knew. Everyone does, although it's supposed to be a secret."

"I don't know, Marie," Kincaid said, sitting beside her. "I don't know, but I surely would like to. Tell me about it, please. Tell me all about it."

And she did. The fire burned to golden embers. The warm, still night grew darker and Marie Lacklander told the tale, her voice soft, her eyes animated.

"Prospectors have been in and out of here for years," she told them, "but no one ever hit much. All the activity was in the Black Hills, over east."

"True," Shy put in. "I never heard of any gold strikes along the Belle Fourche."

"Until this past spring," Marie said, and her voice rose with excitement.

"What happened then?" Matt inquired.

"It was a wet spring, as you know," she went on, "and

85

the Belle Fourche was roaring. The Danby too, being a tributary." She looked anxiously toward her father's tent. The lamp had long ago been put out.

"You can tell us," Matt said encouragingly.

"Well, it was supposed to be a secret."

"Whatever it was, it doesn't seem that it's a secret any-more—to anyone but me."

"No," she said nervously, "it isn't. The spring washout cut away the banks upriver, right where Clive Scales's claim is, and when the rain had stopped, they happened on it."

"On what?" Matt asked with some impatience.

"Why, the coffin, of course! The spring wash had gouged the banks away and left the coffin high and dry. The miner," she said, leaning forward, her voice low, "and his poke were inside."

"Gold dust?"

"Exactly!" Marie's face was fire-bright. She tilted her head nearer to Kincaid and went on, "What happened—what must have happened—is that two prospectors hit something big. A long while back—it must have been a long while back, or everyone would know about it. Anyway, they found dust and a good deal of it. The poke was full. One of them died, apparently—probably the Indians got him, although it could have been anything.

"His partner," Marie said excitedly, her voice a hissing whisper, "must have had to get out. Maybe the Indians were still prowling; it seems likely. Not wanting to risk losing the gold, he buried it with his partner, figuring it would be safer than taking it with him.

"The Sioux were prowling this area then, and so the second man took off, leaving his partner and the gold buried along the Danby.

"But he never made it back. Maybe the Sioux got him. Maybe he broke a leg, maybe his horse threw him. Who knows?" Marie said. "But he never got back. The secret was lost—or would have been, forever, but for the spring flood." She sat back, looking guilty and excited both.

"And that is what started all this?" Matt asked.

"Certainly! That much gold, why, it was enough to get people moving."

"How much was it, exactly?"

"I don't know. Pounds and pounds."

"Then Scales found it?" Matt wanted to know, recalling that it was Scales who had his claim at the point where the banks had collapsed.

"No. Not Scales personally, you see," Marie said. "Of course he knew. He had seen the coffin."

"But not the gold?" Matt persisted.

"Well, I don't know. Two other men found that and took it. They sold the claim to Clive Scales. The body was reburied and the coffin is stored in the back of the Diamond Glen right now. Anyone can see it."

"But the gold, Marie!" Kincaid took her hands and looked intently at her eyes. *"Who* saw the gold?"

"Well"—she was hesitant—"no one that I know of. Or everyone, I don't know. Everyone just *knows!*"

Kincaid looked around, catching Olsen's eye. Everyone knew. It wouldn't be the first gold rush to be started in this way. Everyone knew there was gold here, they had to believe it, or admit they were fools out chasing rainbows. Everyone knew—but where was the goddamned gold? What had brought these men here? What was holding Monument together?

"I want to see that coffin," Matt said quietly.

"But there's nothing left to see," Marie responded.

"Maybe not. But I want to see it. I will see it."

"It's in the Diamond Glen, sir," Olsen reminded him. "Maybe Toomey wouldn't like a visit so much."

"I don't care if it's buried in the middle of the street," Matt said. "I want to see it. Something stinks in Monument, stinks like a twice-buried corpse. Something is wrong here, and I wouldn't care what it was, except people are dying because of it. Let's dig this all up again, Sergeant. Let's dig it up, and try to put it to rest one final time."

seven _____

Malone was doing his own investigating, as was Lieutenant Dunwoodie. Neither was having a great deal of luck—at least not the sort of luck they were expecting.

Malone was out before sunrise, and as the yellow, challenging ball of the sun chinned itself above the horizon, shooting out piercing rays of yellow light, promising yet another unrelentingly hot day, Malone began slowly to search the quadrant, using as his base point the spot where Trueblood had been shot at.

Malone himself was getting the jitters. It wasn't exactly a cheering thought that he was spending more time close to this bastard than anyone else. And suppose there was more than one? Suppose a dozen gun-happy, whiskey-primed Cheyenne took it in their heads to start shooting at Malone?

"Shit," he said unhappily. Taylor had hung around for a time, making it clear that he and the captain expected Malone to find some trace of the sniper—or snipers.

No one had told him how to go about doing it.

He moved with infinite patience across the dry grass plains, his eyes alert to every stone, shadow, and stick. A lizard suddenly darting away seemed as large as a horse, every buffalo turd was something requiring investigation. How in hell Windy Mandalian had ever made a career out of this was beyond Malone. The man must have supernatural eyes. Whatever he had, Malone wished to God that Windy was there right now.

By ten o'clock the plains were a blazing inferno, and Malone had to tug his hat low and squint to see anything at all but the glare. He stopped for water too frequently, trying inefficiently to replace the moisture his body was losing.

Glancing up once, he saw Mr. Taylor near the outpost, watching him hopefully; but Malone had nothing to report and so he turned away, pretending he had not seen the officer at all.

He wondered if Cohen would give him a pass that evening, decided it was possible, and wondered if that Mae Chambers was still working at the Lucky Devil Saloon in town. Some drummer had offered to marry her, and she swore she was going to take him up on it. It would be a shame if she did . . .

Malone found a casing. He squatted down and picked it up, throwing it away angrily. It was a Springfield .45-70, army issue, months old, dulled by exposure to weather.

He nearly stepped on the rattler. A young one, not even eighteen inches long, it was nevertheless deadly. Malone backed away and drew his pistol. Slowly he holstered it again. If he shot the snake, he would have forty armed men rushing out of the post. Then Malone would have to stand there and explain, no it wasn't the sniper, only a rattler, boys.

He detoured, looking for a rock to heave at it. By the time he found one, the rattler was gone.

Nothing—there was nothing out here to be found. No man tracks, horse tracks, flattened grass, cartridge cases, nothing.

Malone was reluctant to go in and report that. The captain hadn't been too pleased the last time. He went to his horse, unlooped one of the two canteens and drenched his head with canteen water, then started again, combing the prairie inch by inch.

A wagon moved slowly across the plains. The fire detail was out scouring the prairie for buffalo chips. Bill Fox was with it, and Rafferty, Dobbs, and Amos Brandt. Brandt kept looking at Fox, his eyes threatening.

"I haven't forgotten that bucket of water," the big man growled.

Rafferty heard the threat and looked up, a buffalo chip in each hand. Amazingly, Fox laughed. But then, Bill had been laughing a lot lately. He was getting sunbaked.

Rafferty felt as if he were going to go nuts from the heat himself. His clothes were soaked clean through with sweat. His eyes were red, raw, weary. He tried to chase all thoughts of the heat away. He moved along steadily, tossing chips into the rolling wagon. The weather had to break—it had to! Fox was giggling crazily and Brandt was muttering, muttering.

"I haven't forgotten that bucket of water, Fox, damn you, I haven't forgotten it by a long shot. You can't throw water on Amos Brandt, by God, and expect him to just forget it, because by God I haven't, Fox . . ."

Rafferty screwed up his face, sighed, and looked to the dry, merciless heavens for help. Fox giggled.

Dinner was a disaster. At noon, with the sun high and motionless in a white sky, Rafferty, Fox, and the fire detail headed in for their meal. Malone was on their heels. Inside the post, everyone was in motion toward the grub hall. There wasn't a whole lot to look forward to in your average day—sleep, maybe a beer if you weren't broke, and mail, which seldom came. But there was always the simple pleasure of eating.

Dutch Rothausen was a big, bluff, red-faced man with a short temper and a nasty disposition, but he could cook. He had once said he knew six hundred ways to prepare buffalo meat—exaggeration, no doubt, but the man was a genius in the kitchen. He could make pies out of dried apples that would melt in your mouth; your mother couldn't have touched Dutch Rothausen's cooking.

Maybe it was the heat, the sullen, somber, everlasting heat. Dutch moved in a trance. The kitchen was a hundred and thirty degrees easily, and Dutch spent twelve hours a day in there.

McBride had caught up with Rafferty, and they went into the grub hall with Fox, Dobbs, and Brandt. Brandt was still muttering, his voice barely audible.

"If you think I've forgotten about that bucket of water, Fox, you're crazy. If you think Amos Brandt will ever forget something like that..."

McBride looked at Rafferty with sympathy. "Is he like that all day?"

"Damned near, Reb."

Fox was close to Brandt now, walking in a curious, crooked crouch, his hands gesturing, his head tilted toward Brandt, listening. Then suddenly he broke into a wild cackling, clapping his hands together. Brandt was crimson and his

92

muttering continued. "Sure, laugh, you lunatic, if you think I'll forget what you did..."

McBride looked at each of them, then put his hand on Rafferty's shoulder, nodding toward the corner of the grub hall. "Let's sit over there."

Dobbs went with them. Sweat trickled down his throat. This was the hottest place on the post. Heat from outside rolled through the door and windows. Heat from the kitchen fires swept through the room.

"Jesus!" Stretch Dobbs muttered. He dabbed at his face with a scarf and sat down without going through the grub line. How they could eat at all was beyond him. He had to borrow a nickel from someone, had to have himself a beer. That wasn't all that was bothering Stretch. His week of guard duty was coming up next. He was six foot seven and was well aware of what sort of target he would make in the twilight.

Armstrong and Trueblood looked like walking death these days. Hollis hadn't gotten over being shot at yet. Rafferty plopped down beside Stretch, and McBride joined them.

"If you think I'll forget what you did, Fox...!" Brandt's voice rose above the general clamor. Stretch closed his eyes.

"Jesus Christ!"

Reb McBride yelled first and spit out his mouthful of food. He snatched up his coffee cup and drained it. Stretch looked at him, saw the sour expression, the disbelief on Reb's face.

"What is it?" Stretch asked.

Rafferty followed suit. He spit out the food in his mouth and grabbed wildly for his cup. "Salt!" Rafferty said, jabbing a finger at his plateful of food. "Damn it! Rothausen's salted the potatoes too much."

Stretch had done some cooking at home, and he looked

skeptically at both men, saying, "It's damned near impossible to oversalt potatoes."

"Well, I guess it ain't!" Rafferty insisted. He offered Stretch a taste. Dobbs took a small bite, but he could still hardly force it down.

"Christ," Dobbs murmured, "it tastes like it was made a pound of salt to a pound of potatoes."

There was a general murmur of protest now. Rafferty, trying to find something worth eating, was failing rapidly. The beef was beyond consumption, the grits just as bad. Salt—everything was salty, inedible, and the murmur of complaint turned into an uproar.

"What are you trying to do, poison us?"

"I can't eat this slop!"

Malone, beat and battered by the heat, had just come in the door, and he held up, astonished. Men were standing and shouting, someone threw a plate on the floor. A soldier grunted like a pig.

"You're crazy, Rothausen!"

"If you think I'll forget that bucket of water, Fox, you're sadly mistaken!"

Malone looked around in blank puzzlement, decided he wasn't as hungry as he had thought, and slipped back out, closing the door carefully behind him. The first shirt was coming on the run, and Malone, on an unhappy inspiration, called out, "Hey, Sarge, how about a pass for tonight?"

Cohen almost bowled him over as he rushed the kitchen door, and his answer was a quick, muttered comment on Malone's parentage.

Malone was too dazed to be angry. The heat—it never let up. He paused, standing on the parade, hat tilted back on his head, wondering just what in hell he had been thinking of when he volunteered to become a soldier.

Then he walked to that hammer-head bay and stepped into leather, the horse nipping at his leg. He turned the horse and rode out once again. He had a long afternoon ahead of him, searching the empty plains. And already he knew he would find nothing.

The dogs yapped at their heels, the naked kids ran after them. Lieutenant Dunwoodie mopped his forehead and looked around him at the transient Indian settlement that had sprouted up beyond the deadline. Here the "friendlies" had settled, some of them—people who had seen too much war and wanted no more. There was no place safer on the plains than here, next to the army outpost. Here they remained, living their silent, sometimes secretive lives.

"What now, Corporal?" Dunwoodie asked Wojensky, who had reined in beside him.

"I was thinking we should talk to Windy Mandalian's woman first, sir. His present woman, that is." Wojensky suppressed a smile. Old Windy, who appeared to be nothing but sinew and buckskin-colored hide, must have had something more appealing. He had had a string of squaws in Tipi Town, as it was called, and they loved him. They loved him while they had him, loved him when he was gone.

In his own way, Windy was the smartest man Wojensky had run into on these broad, lonesome plains.

"What's her name?" Dunwoodie asked, still mopping his perspiration-drenched flesh.

"This one is Quiet Eyes," Wojensky told the junior officer. "I believe that's her tent over there." The corporal nodded toward a tipi set to one side of the camp.

They found the woman doing needlework. A porcupine-quill needle flashed in her deft hands as she stitched beadwork onto a elkskin shirt. When they drew back the flap to the tipi, her brown eyes lifted expectantly, then, seeing that she did not know them, they dropped again to her work.

"Quiet Eyes?" Dunwoodie tried, but the woman didn't even look up. He shrugged at Wojensky, who stepped closer now and tried his luck.

Speaking in a combination of pidgin English, pulverized Cheyenne, and sign language, Wojenksy managed to work his way through a brief interview.

"We're friends of Windy Mandalian's, maybe you've seen me before,"

"Yes," Quiet Eyes said, "I've seen you with my man. What do you want?" Her wide face was unreadable. Her graceful fingers stitched beads without hesitation.

"Well," Wojensky said, "there's been some trouble at the post. Someone shooting at the soldiers. It happens at twilight."

"I've heard shots."

"Someone will be killed. Windy is not here to track them down. We don't know who it is. Do the Cheyenne know who is shooting at our soldiers?"

"I don't know," Quiet Eyes said.

"Does anyone in the camp?"

"I don't know."

"It could be a bad thing for the Cheyenne. Someone might think that the people here are doing it."

"No one here would do that!" Quiet Eyes said, missing a stitch in her anger.

"What did she say, Corporal?" Dunwoodie interrupted. He was staring at the woman as if he believed that by staring hard enough, he could understand her tongue.

"She says she doesn't know anything about the sniper," Wojensky replied.

"Press her on it, man," Dunwoodie said.

"Yes, sir." Wojensky returned his attention to the squaw. "Now, Quiet Eyes, someone must have seen something. Maybe someone has an idea why this is happening. Who can we talk to?"

"I don't know," she said shortly. "I didn't do it. I don't know who did it. I don't know who to talk to."

Wojensky tried a time longer, phrasing his questions differently, but it was obvious that Quiet Eyes either knew nothing or was going to say nothing. Wojensky turned and shrugged.

"Dead end here, sir," he said. Wojensky almost had the idea that Quiet Eyes thought she was protecting Windy by saying nothing at all. Maybe she thought that, maybe she didn't. At any rate, she wasn't going to open up to Wojensky. "Maybe we'd better try someone else, sir."

"All right," Dunwoodie agreed. He wondered if he wasn't agreeing just to escape the heat of the tipi. It was close and musty in there. Outside it was no better. Hot, oppressive, barely endurable.

"Now what?" the officer asked.

"Start through the village—take 'em one by one, I suppose," Wojensky said.

"Yes." Dunwoodie looked at the bleached skies, wiped his forehead again, and sighed. "Try everyone who will speak to us, I suppose."

They started through the camp, followed by dogs and kids. Brown eyes lifted to meet them, grim mouths answered Wojensky's questions hesitantly. They were an hour interviewing three men, and Dunwoodie, his nerves frayed by the heat, was growing impatient.

"Let's split up, Corporal," he suggested. "I'll take the tipis west of here. Most of them seem to have enough English to understand what I'm asking."

97

"Whatever you say, sir," Wojensky answered. He too wanted only to get out of here, and their progress was painfully slow.

Wojensky walked off and Dunwoodie saw him rap on a tipi pole and be summoned in to disappear behind the flap. The young officer himself strode toward the nearest tipi, leading his horse. Oddly, he found himself thinking of Sheila, only Sheila and those soft eyes, that soft young body of hers.

And here he was, stuck, while she grew fretful in Cheyenne. He lifted a hand and tapped on a tipi pole. A voice answered and he took it for an invitation to enter. Lifting the flap, he stepped inside.

Sitting on their haunches inside the tipi were three men, two of them quite old, the third of middle years, lean as a fencerail, with black, black eyes and a scarred face. Two women sat in the shadows doing some domestic work that Dunwoodie could not identify in the darkness of the tipi.

"Good afternoon," Dunwoodie said clearly. "I am investigating an incident that occurred nearby . . ."

A spate of rapid Cheyenne interrupted the little speech.

"Who you?" the man with the scar asked.

"Dunwoodie," the officer replied promptly. The man had savage eyes. His badly scarred, lean face was that of a warrior. Dunwoodie wondered what he had walked into. He wished suddenly that Wojensky were there.

The men spoke together. One of them held three sticks in his hands. They were squared off and painted different colors on each side.

"Sit, Dunwoodie," the scarred man said. The women, only their eyes and hands visible in the shadows, watched him.

"I really didn't come to—" Dunwoodie started to argue, then realized that perhaps it would be a serious breach of etiquette not to sit. Wojensky had cautioned him to smoke if a pipe was offered. "You won't get anything at all out of 'em if you're standoffish," the corporal had said. "You're in their homes, so it's best to follow their ways."

Simple, sound advice, Dunwoodie had thought. Yet he wasn't anxious to stay here. He wanted to ask his questions and get out.

"Sit, Dunwoodie," the man repeated, and he watched with obsidian eyes as Dunwoodie moved nearer and crouched down as they were doing. All three braves were staring at him now. One man grinned toothlessly. Dunwoodie had a sudden uncomfortable twinge—suppose this man, the one with the scarred face, was the sniper? Or worse.

Wojensky had told him that sometimes hostiles would sneak into the camp to hide. The man had a butcher's face. Friendly he might be, but there had been a time when the man was a warrior. There definitely had been a time...

"What I wish to ask..." Dunwoodie began. Sweat trickled down his nose.

"I am Blue Hand," Scarface said. "This is Two Sticks, this is High Top Mountain."

"I'm pleased, gentlemen. Blue Hand, I'm here to investigate—"

Blue Hand cut him off again. "Here. You see?" The Cheyenne took the colored sticks from High Top Mountain's hand and tossed them on the floor before Dunwoodie.

"Uh, yes," Dunwoodie said. What was that supposed to mean?

"Very good. Very good." Blue Hand said.

"I want to know if you have seen anyone shooting at soldiers."

"You have a dollar?" Blue Hand asked.

Would he have to buy information? Dunwoodie dug into

his pocket. Small price to pay, he thought. He placed the dollar before him, and Blue Hand nodded.

"Good." He then collected the three sticks and handed them to Dunwoodie. He motioned with his hand for Dunwoodie to throw them, and the officer did so.

What is this? he wondered. Were they asking the spirits if it was good to speak to the white man? The sticks clattered to a halt, two of them showing blue, the third white. Blue Hand grunted. High Top Mountain laughed. They seemed pleased by the omen, Dunwoodie thought.

Blue Hand certainly was. He handed Dunwoodie a muskrat pelt. "For you."

"Thank you. It's a fine gift," Dunwoodie said, touching the fur. Wojensky had said that it was customary to exchange gifts.

"Good." Blue Hand passed him the sticks once more.

"What, again?"

Blue Hand nodded and Dunwoodie rolled the sticks again, and again High Top Mountain barked a laugh. Was that a good sign too? It was time to get down to business, Dunwoodie thought. But Blue Hand was not through with his ritual of friendship.

"This. For you." Blue Elk handed Dunwoodie two more pelts.

"I can't accept these," Dunwoodie protested. "They're very fine presents, but really, there's no need."

"Good." Blue Hand again handed the lieutenant the sticks. How long would this go on? Shrugging mentally, Dunwoodie tossed the sticks again.

Two red and one white. Blue Elk's face was unreadable. He turned and said something to the women, and the older of them brought a pile of pelts forward. She dropped them beside Dunwoodie without a word.

"This is really too much! Quite unnecessary, my friend. I only wished to ask if you might have seen anyone shooting at soldiers, or perhaps heard reports of such an incident."

"Good." Blue Hand pressed the sticks into Dunwoodie's hand again and he watched as Dunwoodie simply held them.

The officer looked around him uncomprehendingly The warriors were simply watching, sitting crouched, arms draped over their knees.

"Listen, what is this?" Dunwoodie asked, gesturing toward the furs. "I really can't accept them." He jabbed an emphatic finger at the furs and shrugged. "Doesn't anyone here speak English?"

Blue Hand pointed at the furs as well, and then turned toward the corner where the women sat. He growled something and the younger rose.

"Ah, the translator at last," Dunwoodie thought.

The woman came forward, and he was surprised to see a fine-looking young woman with glossy dark hair, a broad mouth, and high cheekbones. She was really remarkably attractive. She stood behind Blue Hand and he jabbed his finger at her, saying something Dunwoodie could not get.

"If you could explain, young lady," Dunwoodie said, starting to rise, "I would appreciate it."

"No." Blue Hand put a hand on Dunwoodie's shoulder and forced him down again. He shoved the sticks into the lieutenant's hand.

"No, really. Not again," Dunwoodie cried. "I only wanted to ask about the sniper."

"Good." Blue Hand's voice was toneless. He gestured as before, urging Dunwoodie to roll the sticks.

"Young lady—" Dunwoodie began, but Blue Hand interrupted him harshly. Those black eyes were smoldering now, and Dunwoodie had the idea that he had better do as

101

the Cheyenne asked. He tossed the sticks. Three blues. The warrior slapped his head in disgust and stood, shoving the girl toward Dunwoodie.

The game was over then, etiquette satisfied. Dunwoodie stood as well, speaking to Blue Hand, who had his back turned. "Now then, if you have heard anything about these incidents, I would be appreciative if you could relate that information to me."

The man said nothing. The girl was looking at him appraisingly. A wedge of light appeared on the tipi floor, and Dunwoodie turned to see Wojensky standing there.

"Ah, good. I'm having a hell of a time here, Corporal. The man won't speak to me, and I'm wondering if he isn't concealing something."

"I'll ask him, sir," Wojensky volunteered. He glanced at the young woman and at the furs, his eyebrows knitting together.

Dunwoodie stood, arms folded, as Wojensky spoke to the Cheyenne. Blue Hand snapped an answer, and Wojensky turned to stare at his lieutenant.

"What is it?" Dunwoodie asked, but Wojensky held up a hand. He asked Blue Hand another question, and with much waving of his arms, Blue Hand responded.

Wojensky turned slowly then, his face blank, his eyes vaguely amused.

"Well, what is it, Wojensky? Does he know anything? What does he have to say?"

"He doesn't know anything about the sniping, sir," Wojensky answered with reluctance.

"Then what . . . ?"

Wojensky stepped nearer. "Pick up your furs, sir, and let's get out of here. Blue Hand's in a dark mood."

"Pick up my furs?" Dunwoodie was puzzled. "Why? What's going on here? Why did he give me those furs?"

"The sticks, sir. Didn't you know? You were gambling with Blue Hand, and you won those furs from him."

"Gambling! Look, Wojensky. Tell him I didn't know, tell him I don't want the furs."

"I can't do that, sir. It's an insult." Wojensky's voice was quite serious. "You can't give them back."

"This is absurd. Look, just tell him I don't want them."

"It's not possible, sir, believe me. You'd be insulting him terribly. Blue Hand was gambling seriously, and if I were you I'd take my winnings and git."

"This can't be all that important," Dunwoodie said in an urgent whisper.

"It is, sir," Wojensky assured him. "It's most serious to Blue Hand. Serious enough that he wagered his best wife."

"He what?"

"He wagered his second wife," Wojensky said. "He says he offered to play her against the furs, and you took him up on it. There she is, sir," Wojensky said, nodding at the young woman beside Dunwoodie. "And she's all yours."

eight _____

Lieutenant Max Dunwoodie didn't speak for a long minute. He couldn't. Nothing he had heard made sense. He was a player in some absurd farce. He attempted a laugh and made a dry, gasping sound.

"Tell them, Corporal," he said, gripping Wojensky's arm tightly. "Tell them that I didn't know, that I don't want the furs or the girl!"

Dunwoodie was panicked, Blue Hand somber. The girl smiled bashfully. Wojensky muttered something to Blue Hand and the warrior responded angrily, waving his arm in a motion even Dunwoodie could interpret. He wanted them gone.

"Tell him I'll play him again, for whatever he wants," Dunwoodie insisted, still clutching Wojensky's arm.

"What if you win again, sir?"

"Christ, I can't win every time, can I? I don't even know what I'm doing."

Wojensky spoke to Blue Hand. The response was terse. "Says he don't want to gamble anymore, sir," the corporal translated. "Says all he's got is his buffalo pony, the tipi, and his other wife. With winter coming on, he can't afford to lose none of 'em."

"For God's sake, man!" Dunwoodie said, stepping toward Blue Hand, rising panic flooding his chest. "I don't want the furs, I don't want your wife!"

"Go!" The word was a command, not a request, and Wojensky, sizing things up, offered his advice.

"I think we'd best get out of here, sir. There has been trouble in such situations."

"But how in blazes—what am I supposed to do with the woman?"

"I don't know, but we'd better scoot. Maybe when Mandalian comes back he can straighten this all out—he's got influence here. He's gotten himself related to half these folks. But for now"—Wojensky nodded his head toward the exit—"we'd best git."

"This is absurd!"

"So's gettin' our heads bashed in over it, sir."

There was no answer to that. Dunwoodie, feeling the fool, watched as the girl hugged the other woman, hastily packed some belongings, and then shouldered the bundle of furs.

Blue Hand was still staring at them as they slipped from the tipi and Dunwoodie mounted his horse. Wojensky followed, the woman bringing up the rear.

In the daylight, Dunwoodie could see that she was indeed a fine-looking woman, long-legged, high-breasted, with healthy skin and good teeth. He looked at Wojensky, wanting to know what to do, how to extricate himself from this ridiculous situation. The corporal only shrugged, and damn him! He was smiling faintly.

"Let's play it straight for now, sir. Windy'll be able to straighten this out."

"Will he?" Dunwoodie's voice was brittle. Why in God's name was he here? How had this happened? He belonged in Cheyenne, walking down the aisle with his Sheila. Instead he was on these dreary plains, at this miserable outpost, with a squaw following him along. A squaw he had won tossing sticks!

Dunwoodie tried not to look back, but from time to time he caught sight of her from the corner of his eye. A dark-haired, dark-eyed woman in buckskins, carrying a bundle of pelts on her back.

"All right, Wojensky," Dunwoodie hissed, "what now? What in God's name do I do now! I can't simply march into the BOQ and say, 'Hello, Mr. Taylor. Meet my squaw.' Then I could go to the captain, tell him all about this. And be a laughingstock the rest of my career! They'd tell tales about the green shavetail who gambled for a squaw without even knowing what he was doing. What will my fiancée say, for God's sake. What do I do, Wojensky? What *can* I do?" Dunwoodie's expression changed to panic. "Don't say a word, Corporal. That's an order! Please!"

Jesus, all the men would know. Dunwoodie would be a joke. His very name would set the men to hysterics. His entire career was on the line! Wojensky was reassuring.

"Don't worry about it, sir. This happens all the time— various sorts of misunderstandings, that is. Not that I've heard of this particular problem cropping up before," he said thoughtfully, "but there's always some problems when different cultures come together."

"But how can I get out of this?" Dunwoodie demanded.

The woman was still marching along behind them. She smiled as Dunwoodie looked at her. "Is she my wife or what?"

"Yes, sir, she is your wife. But don't worry, I'm sure Mandalian can get you out of this. As for the rest of it—I won't talk to nobody about this." *Even an officer deserves a break,* Wojensky thought. The man was green, but he wasn't snotty or high-handed like some shavetails Wo had seen. He wished it had happened to some of them. Hell, Dunwoodie wasn't bad at all. He'd probably be a good officer one day, if he kept the right men under him. It was too easy now, too cheap to expose him to ridicule.

Wojensky drew his horse up. "I don't reckon we'd better go any nearer the post until you decide just what you want to do, sir."

"What I want to do?" Dunwoodie waved a hand in the air. "What *can* I do?" The woman had stopped when they stopped, and she stood there smiling faintly, the bundle of furs still on her back.

"I'll talk to her. I'll tell her to stay here. She'll do it, and that'll be good enough for now."

"Out here?" Dunwoodie looked around at the sunbaked plains. The outpost stood gaunt and stolid against the barren earth. Behind them the cones of Tipi Town dotted the dry prairie.

"She wouldn't mind, sir. Really. She's spent most all her life on these plains."

"But where would she stay—how would she eat?"

"That is something else again. I reckon it'll be up to you to provide for her in some way until we can get this straightened out. It shouldn't be too much of a problem to smuggle some grub out to her."

"No. No, I suppose not. I guess I'll have to do that," Dunwoodie said miserably. "Go ahead."

"Sir?"

"Go ahead and tell her. Tell her to stay. Tell her I'll be back with some food. After dark."

"Yes, sir."

Wojensky rattled out some Cheyenne. Apparently it wasn't too good, because the woman asked him to repeat it. Finally, with much pointing and gesturing, Wojensky managed to get the point across.

She looked up at Dunwoodie with wide, hurt eyes, but she sat, dropping the bundle of furs beside her. She just sat there looking at him. Dunwoodie looked into her eyes and then had to turn his head away in embarrassment. The woman was now counting on him, he realized. She had been traded to this white soldier, and now her life was dependent on him. He must provide, he must build a shelter and bring meat. She was at his disposal and quite uncertain.

"Tell her I have to see about shelter, about hunting for buffalo," Dunwoodie told his corporal, and Wojensky blinked. "Tell her," the lieutenant repeated more quietly.

Wojensky did so, and that seemed to satisfy the woman. She leaned back against the bundle of furs, smiling at them as they turned their horses toward the outpost.

"Well, it wouldn't do to have her think I was just riding off and leaving her," Dunwoodie said.

"No, sir."

"I mean, I couldn't do that."

"No, sir. You're quite right."

Dunwoodie was silent until they had nearly reached the gate, and then he said, "If you ever tell anyone—anyone!— I'll find a way to get even, Wojensky. I swear it."

"I won't talk, sir. I said I wouldn't, and I won't."

Dunwoodie looked at Wojensky and read his eyes. Then, satisfied, he nodded and they rode in through the gates of Outpost Number Nine, Dunwoodie sparing only a single backward glance for the slender, dark-eyed woman who sat alone on the vast plains, watching after her man.

The summary meeting was held in Captain Conway's office at four in the afternoon. Present were Lieutenants Taylor and Dunwoodie, and Corporal Wojensky and Private Malone.

The room was dead hot. The window, though flung wide, admitted no breeze. Malone was sunburned, and his uniform was white with the salt of his perspiration.

Warner Conway offered no drinks, no preliminaries. He wanted to know what was happening with this sniper action, and he wanted to know immediately.

His question brought a chorus of mumbling and a lot of throat-clearing. Conway frowned.

"Mr. Taylor?"

"Sir, I directed Private Malone to search the area from where it is assumed Private Trueblood was sniped at, and unfortunately . . ."

"Nothing, Malone?"

Malone looked up, gritting his teeth. A lot had been expected of him, but he had produced nothing. "No, sir, I guess I ain't enough of a tracker. Either that, or we got a plains-wise, heap savvy man out there. There is *nothing*. I done my best," Malone said, somewhat shamefaced. His last words were more of a mumble than a coherent statement.

"All right." Conway looked at Malone with flinty eyes. The burly private's reputation was appalling. He was a drinker, a brawler, a troublemaker in the grand Irish tradition. But Conway had never yet heard anyone intimate that Malone didn't do his best on post, on duty. If he said he had done his best, he probably had. It was no consolation.

"Mr. Dunwoodie?"

110

Dunwoodie nearly jumped from his seat. Malone and Taylor glanced at him in amazement. Captain Conway frowned in surprise.

"Yes, sir?"

"Your report, Dunwoodie. Any luck at all down in Tipi Town?"

"Uh . . ." Dunwoodie's voice faltered. "Luck? No one we interviewed, sir, seemed to have any information to impart, sir. Corporal Wojensky? No information?" Dunwoodie looked as if he was ready to crack. His cheeks were flushed red over pallor. His eyes were unnaturally bright. Conway frowned. The heat seemed to be getting to everyone. He had already had to call Dutch Rothausen on the carpet this afternoon.

"Nothing," Wojensky said very hastily. He grinned sheepishly and turned his eyes downward.

"Then we have nothing," Warner Conway said, his voice steely. He glanced again at his men. Dunwoodie appeared ready to faint; Malone was obviously sun-battered. Wojensky was fidgeting on his chair, his eyes turned down. Taylor's expression was absolutely blank.

"We have nothing," Conway repeated. "Why is that, gentlemen? *Have* we got a ghost out there? A man who wants to kill soldiers is what we have, and as yet none of you has been able to produce a single fragment of evidence!" Conway's hand slammed down against his desk.

"I won't have this, men. I won't stand for it. We can find nothing." He looked at Malone. "We can get nothing from the Cheyenne, although they have eyes like hawks and know what we've had for breakfast on this post." He glared at Dunwoodie and Wojensky now. The captain was obviously hot about this.

"Sir, when Windy gets back—" Mister Taylor began.

The captain cut him short. "When Windy gets back!

Damn it, I admire Windy as much as anyone. His skills are remarkable. But are you all trying to tell me that we can do nothing without him? Do you mean that without this civilian tracker, our force is ineffective, helpless, unable even to protect itself? In that event, gentlemen, we are in poor shape and we haven't got much justification for representing ourselves as a military force, have we? Perhaps I should step down and let Windy take over my desk."

There was a murmur of disavowal. Conway was hot, and there was no sense in saying anything. He stood, placed himself before a map of the territory, and was silent for a long minute.

"All this area," Conway said, sweeping his palm across the map, "and we maintain its security, protect the settlers, the transients. And yet we are not secure in our own fortifications. I am not happy with this, gentlemen. I want you to get back to your work, I want you to find this man, or his sign, or his motive, or... anything."

They rose, all trying to become invisible, apparently, and Conway, with an immense sigh, ran his hand across his brow. "I'm as hot and as weary as you men are. Let's have a drink."

"Enlisted too?" Malone asked, brightening.

"This once," Conway said. He hadn't enough glasses, but the coffee mugs Ben Cohen brought in were good enough. Conway poured them all two fingers, and as he lifted his glass to them he requested, "Don't mention this, gentlemen. I'd hate to have the entire post think I'm going soft."

"No, sir," they all muttered in somber agreement, but they smiled inwardly at the idea of anyone thinking the captain was going soft.

Outside, Malone stretched his arms and squinted with frustration at the bleached sky. The sun, slowly wheeling westward, jabbed at his eyes mockingly.

He gathered up the reins of his horse and walked it to the paddock, where he unsaddled it. Fox was there, also unsaddling a horse. He looked at Malone, shook his head, and said, "Jesus, it's hot."

Malone decided it would be better not to say anything. He carried his saddle through the alleyway that led back toward the interior of the post, and went into the tack shed, where he met Rafferty and learned about the disaster at dinner.

He shook his head. "Well," he said, "if the heat's got to Dutch, this is *hot.*"

Stepping out of the musty, shadowed shed into the harsh daylight, they saw Reb McBride hunkered on his heels. McBride lifted a hand and touched his finger to his lips.

"What in hell . . . ?" Then Rafferty saw Brandt. The big man was pressed against the wall of the shed, his dark eyes gleeful.

"What's going on?" Rafferty whispered as they joined the bugler.

"You'll see."

Malone saw nothing except Brandt standing by the water trough, his hands clenching and unclenching with some secret pleasure. Then they saw him tense and hold absolutely still.

Around the corner came Bill Fox, carrying his saddle. He had seen Rafferty, Malone, and McBride, and his eyes opened wider in silent curiosity. Then he hit something with his foot, stumbled, lost the saddle, and took a header into the trough.

Brandt broke into a wild war dance. Fox was fuming, soaking wet, lying with his arms splayed in the watering trough, his curses filling the air.

Brandt leaped and performed a crazy jig, taunting Fox.

113

"You thought I'd forget, didn't you, Fox? Amos Brandt never forgets a man who does him dirty. I didn't forget that bucket of water!"

Fox was sullen, silent. He pulled himself out of the trough and looked back at the tripwire that Brandt had rigged.

Fox stood like a scarecrow for a long minute, his uniform pasted to his body, his hair over his eyes. Then, snatching up his hat and saddle, he turned and squished off toward the shed, saying nothing as Brandt danced and jeered behind him.

"Jesus," Malone muttered. "Crazier and crazier. And you sit and watch it," he said shaking his head.

"Hell," McBride said, rising, "I didn't know what Brandt was up to. I just knew something was cooking."

"They'll kill each other," Rafferty predicted.

"No. Did you see Fox's face? He's finished. There's no way he can top that one anyway. He'll have to admit that Brandt won."

They met Trueblood at the barracks. He was pale, unsteady on his feet. His eyes had dark circles around them.

"Damn, you look like hell," Rafferty said. "Shouldn't you get some sleep?"

"Sleep?" Trueblood just turned his head toward them. "Get some sleep?" He laughed silently, his Adam's apple bobbing, his mouth hung open. Malone and McBride exchanged a worried glance. "Sure—no problem sleeping. Except that it's about a hundred and seventy in here. I've got nothing to keep me awake, nothing but knowing some bastard is likely to shoot my ass off tonight. Hell, maybe he'll hit my head. I'll never know it—just *bam!* And my head explodes like a melon. Unless you all caught him today." He looked at Malone, who could only shake his head. "No, I didn't think so."

"It's only two more nights, Truebood. You can make it."

"Two more?" Stretch Dobbs was lying on his bunk, bathed in sweat. "I thought it was three."

"Two, Stretch."

"Jesus." He lay back.

"He's got the duty next," Rafferty said.

"Maybe I'll come down sick," Dobbs muttered. "Maybe I'll just shoot myself, save the man the trouble."

"I don't think he wants to hit anybody," Malone said, sitting to pull off his boots. "Hell, he's missed twice."

"Would you like risking your neck on that?" Dobbs asked, rolling onto his side.

"No," Malone answered. "No, I guess I wouldn't."

Lieutenant Max Dunwoodie caught up with Taylor at the BOQ, and asked a favor.

"I've got to go off post for an hour or so."

"Oh?" Taylor's eyebrow lifted quizzically.

"Yes." Dunwoodie spoke rapidly, keeping his eyes turned down. "I've got the duty, you know. But I was hoping that you would take an hour for me." He paused. "It's really urgent, Taylor."

"No problem," Taylor answered and Dunwoodie's face relaxed, breaking into a smile. "What's the matter, though, Max? Feel like talking to someone about it? Sometimes it helps."

"Thanks, Taylor, but no. No, I don't think so. But you'll stand for me tonight?" Taylor nodded, and Dunwoodie slapped him on the back. "Thanks. Thanks so much. I won't forget it, Taylor."

"I won't let you," Taylor responded with a grin. But Max Dunwoodie's mind was already somewhere else. He said goodbye absently. Standing on the plankwalk in front of the BOQ, Taylor watched as Dunwoodie crossed the parade rapidly, heading for Pop Evans's place. He walked right past Armstrong and Miller, missing their salute entirely, and Taylor, frowning, turned toward the officers' quarters.

It was an hour before sunset when Max Dunwoodie rode out of Number Nine, a sack of goods over the withers of his horse. He had his hat tipped down over his eyes and he looked neither right nor left as he went out the gate and onto the plains.

Dunwoodie rode due south for a time and then circled back, watching the post. He saw only one man, unidentifiable at this distance. He seemed to be out digging a latrine pit. Punishment? It was late for a work detail.

He pushed that thought aside and rode slowly toward the deadline, hoping. Hoping that the woman, tired and hot, confused, had gone home to her husband. That thought cheered him. Of course she would go home, wouldn't she? Why sit out on the prairie waiting for a man who was nothing to her?

Of course! He loosened up and leaned back in the saddle. The woman had to have more sense than Blue Hand. She would grow tired of this foolishness, and hungry, and would return to her people.

But she hadn't. Twilight was on the plains, and Dunwoodie thought briefly of the sniper. Yet he wasn't able to give it much consideration. His eyes and thoughts were on the woman who sat against the earth, her back to the pile of pelts, her dark eyes watching Dunwoodie's slow approach.

This was absurd—somehow he had to get the message through to her. *Go home*. It was that simple. She surely knew enough English to understand that. He would give her

116

the goods he had purchased at the sutler's and send her on her way.

With determination he swung down from his horse, slipped the sack off the horse's withers, and walked to her. She watched submissively. The shadows of twilight darkened her face. Dunwoodie crouched in front of her, holding out the sack he carried.

"Listen, You can have this. It's all for you, but you must go home, back to your husband." She did not move. "Do you understand?"

She got to her knees and opened the sack eagerly, removing the salt, tinned beef and fruit, flour, and bacon. She examined each item happily.

"Take this"—his gesture included the furs—"and go home. Go back to your husband, Blue Hand."

He saw the flash of a knife and drew back sharply. But she had no intention of harming Dunwoodie. She used the knife to open a tin of peaches, and with delight she turned back the lid and sampled the sticky, sweet fruit. She turned her eyes to him and said something he could not understand.

"There's more in there," Dunwoodie said. "Take it to your husband. Enjoy it. They are gifts for you."

She came suddenly to her knees, and before Dunwoodie knew what was happening, she had thrown her arms around his neck and was kissing him, her mouth sweet and sticky with the peaches, her breasts flattened against him.

"No," he protested, but there was no starch in the complaint. He thought briefly of Sheila, but that thought wasn't enough to stave off need, either. She lay back against the furs, drawing him down with her, and his protest was only a muted whimper.

Twilight was fading to darkness and the plains grew empty, dark. There was no one else on the land, it seemed, there was no reality as Dunwoodie's pulse began to race. No reality but this peach-tasting, earthy woman, his wife. He held back for a moment and then pressed his mouth to hers, and she gave a satisfied murmur.

Her hands were on his fly, Dunwoodie realized with momentary alarm. Alarm gave way to pleasure as her nimble fingers undid the buttons and dipped inside his trousers. Her hands were warm, eager, and they searched him with satisfaction.

Abruptly she rolled away, and Dunwoodie gazed at her in confusion. But it was only for a moment. She rose and pulled her buckskin dress over her head, and there was just enough lingering light for Dunwoodie to make out the outlines of her lush, short body. His heart quickened again, and he thought of Sheila.

Sheila, whose eyes were lusty and bright, who led him on and on and never...Dunwoodie reached up and yanked her to him and she gave a squeal of delight. Darkness folded around them and Dunwoodie kicked out of his clothes. By the time he had accomplished that, the woman, his nameless wife, had made a bed of furs. Dunwoodie crawled to her, sinking into the softness of ermine and fox, into the softness of the woman.

She laughed very quietly, and her hands found his erection, cradling it for a moment, her fingers moving lightly down the shaft, and then she lay back, drawing him to her, and her legs spread widely and lifted. As she eased Dunwoodie into position, her heels rested on his shoulders, her fingers toyed with him, encircled him, stroked him, and then he was within her and she gave a gasp, her hands clenching his buttocks, holding him tightly to her as she purred, as she flooded with fluid warmth.

Dunwoodie was lost in a dizzy warmth, a crazy, sensual web of touch and motion. She swayed against him, battered him with her pelvis. She drew his head to her breats and he nuzzled her there, feeling the soft contours against his cheeks, hearing the banging of her heart, the happy noises she made deep in her throat each time Dunwoodie arched himself and drove deeply into her.

Her hands stroked his hair, rested on his shoulders, and traced patterns on his back. And those hips—they moved constantly, swaying, thrusting, lifting, pitching, as she carried Dunwoodie along on a wild, tumultuous journey through rapids and into deep, madly spinning whirlpools.

She laughed like a child at play, soothing him with her hands, inflaming him with her kisses until Dunwoodie went rigid, his arteries hammering as if they would burst free of his skin, and he flooded her with a hard, frantic climax.

Then he lay beside her. She cooed in his ear, toyed with the hair on his chest. It was fully dark now, but no cooler. She was warm and soft and comforting in the night. He clung to her for a long while.

It was only later, as his pulse slowed, that he gradually felt guilt creeping over him. Sheila! He had cheated on her shamefully. Lying here on the ground with a wild, savage Indian woman. What sort of man was he becoming?

"Look," Dunwoodie said, "this is all wrong. You've got to go home. I'm sorry all of this happened." He slipped away from her and lay on his back, his perspiration-slick body cooling. She rolled to him and bent low, kissing his mouth, her dark hair brushing his cheeks, her breasts grazing his chest.

"You'll just have to go now, all right?" *My God!* he thought suddenly. *What would Blue Hand do if he caught us like this?* "Please?" He gripped her shoulders and she stood.

Dunwoodie had closed his eyes. She would dress and she would go. But when he opened his eyes, she was not gone. She stood over him, silhouetted against the starbright sky. She stood across his hips, and as Dunwoodie watched, she tossed her hair back over her shoulders and squatted down.

"Listen," he began, but his objection was lost as he felt her hands on him. She was squatting low, and she lifted his still swollen erection, touching it to her own warm inner flesh. "Listen..." the argument died in his throat as she began working the head of his shaft around, her face intent. She groaned slightly, and Dunwoodie was flooded with sensation so sweet and demanding that it was almost painful. She rubbed herself against him, using only the tip of his shaft. Her face was lifted to the skies and Dunwoodie, in exquisite agony, reached out and gripped her legs, clawing at her, trying to force her down.

Finally, when he could stand no more, when he thought he would have to throw her aside and take care of business himself, she settled onto him with exquisite ease, burying him within her, and he almost cried out himself, it was so unendurably pleasurable.

She rode him, her head thrown back exultantly, her buttocks sliding over his thighs damply, her body working against his, and within minutes Dunwoodie had reached a second panting orgasm. She lay forward then, gripping his shoulders tightly, and he sighed, closing his eyes in exhaustion. They did not move for a long while. There was only the soft breathing, her hands on his thighs, the close, damp touch of her body.

And then he felt her begin to sway slightly, to grind her pelvis against his, and he put a hand on her buttocks, holding her still.

"No, not again. Please go home." His voice was weak and cracked, his body felt ravaged. But she only smiled, putting a finger to his lips, and then, humming a tuneless little song, she returned to her efforts and Dunwoodie, to his blank astonishment, felt need rising in his loins once more.

nine _____

Where was he? Taylor peered out the BOQ window once more. No sign of Dunwoodie. An hour, he had said, an hour! It had been three already. Where had he gone, anyway? What was the big secret? And what was Taylor supposed to tell the captain if he asked.?

Not that there was anything wrong with this—it was only annoying. When a man says an hour, it should be an hour. It was annoying. Annoying and puzzling.

What was he doing? What *was* there to do out there? Maybe, he reflected, Dunwoodie had some wild plan to trap the twilight sniper. But twilight had come and gone hours ago. Where in hell was he?

Trueblood was at the gate, his mind fuzzy, his eyes heavy. Why was it he only got truly sleepy when he was

123

on guard duty? Maybe it was because it had cooled a bit by nightfall. Who knew—he only knew he was tired, dead tired.

The tension had kept him wide awake that first hour. He knew he had beaten the record again when he made his circuit of the outpost. Damn, he wished they would catch that bastard!

Someone was approaching the gate, and Trueblood pivoted sharply, going to it. He peered out to see Bill Fox walking in.

"Christ, Bill, what are you doing out there?"

"Nothing," Fox hissed back. Then, damn him, he broke into a giggle.

"Bill? Are you all right?" There was dirt all over Fox, and his eyes were glazed.

"Sure. Sure, I'm all right." Fox slipped off toward the barracks, breaking into a laugh again, and Trueblood sighed. He didn't have time to reflect on Fox's behavior. Someone else was approaching, on horseback. He started to challenge, and then saw that it was his duty officer.

Trueblod stepped aside, saluted, and watched as Mr. Dunwoodie rode limply past. His salute was not returned.

Trueblood latched the gate again, wondering what in hell was going on. Were they all going nuts? Fox out there by himself at night, laughing like an idiot. Mr. Dunwoodie—he had been wearing a silly damned grin. His eyes went right through Trueblood. Trueblood didn't think he had even seen him.

He shrugged and shifted his rifle from hand to hand. Maybe Fox had screwed up and Dunwoodie had taken him out to do some digging. Trueblood yawned, suddenly not caring. It was too much effort to think about it. He began a slow, methodical pacing, staring out at the plains, fighting

124

desperately to stay awake. If he fell asleep one more time it was his ass, and he knew it.

That night he had been asleep on his feet—what a break that was. He shuddered, just thinking about it. Trueblood pinched himself hard in the ribs, so hard that it brought tears to his eyes. He would have a nasty bruise there, come morning. But it didn't do a damn thing to wake him up. Miserably he watched the dark prairie through slowly drooping eyes.

"Christ, Dunwoodie, where were you?"

Taylor bounced from his bunk, unpinning the OD armband he was wearing. He handed it to Dunwoodie, who let it dangle from his hand. He yawned.

"Thanks, Taylor."

"Where were you, Dunwoodie?" Taylor demanded. "You said an hour. It's been three and a half."

"Has it? I'm sorry." Dunwoodie was fumbling with the armband, trying to pin it on. The man was obviously exhausted. "Taylor, I am sorry. I'll pull a whole day for you next week, all right?"

"It's not that, Max. I was just concerned. What were you doing?"

"Can't tell you," Dunwoodie said around another prodigious yawn.

"You can't tell me," Taylor said flatly. "Look, is it this sniper business, Max? Have you got some sort of plan?"

Dunwoodie turned thoughtfully toward Taylor. He winked. "Could be, Taylor, could be."

"You watch your butt, man. That man can shoot, whoever he is. You stay low if you're out at twilight."

"I will, Taylor." Dunwoodie started toward the door and then halted, his hand on the knob. "Uh, look, Taylor, I may have to slip out again tomorrow at the same time. At twilight. Maybe you could cover for me again. I'll stand two days for you, whatever you say."

"It's not necessary," Taylor said. "I'll cover for you. But you watch yourself."

"Yes," Dunwoodie said with an odd, crooked smile, "I will. Thanks, Taylor, thanks very much."

Then he was out the door, his gait heavy and loose. Taylor watched him for a minute, wondering if the heat had gotten to Dunwoodie too. Then, with a sigh, he blew out the lamp and lay back on his bunk, staring at the dark ceiling.

Trueblood stiffened to attention, but Dunwoodie walked past him without glancing his way, and Trueblood's eyes narrowed. The man looked tired. He looked like Trueblood felt, and that was poorly.

One more night, Trueblood told himself. One more goddamned night of guard duty and then he could sleep, could forget the sniper. One more night—he yawned—if he made it.

Armstrong was a welcome sight when he came on duty to relieve Trueblood, who nodded wearily at him, and staggered back toward the barracks. He didn't bother to take off his boots. He flopped onto the bunk with his rifle still in his hand. He hit the bunk and closed his eyes.

He closed his eyes, but sleep would not come. Someone was snoring. Fox was giggling. The heat was unbearable. Trueblood turned over, the sweat rolling off him. In frustration he beat his fist against his pillow.

Fox giggled, someone snored. Dobbs mumbled in his sleep. And the night passed in slow, torpid minutes.

Morning brought no relief, physical or mental. The sun was a white glare, the barracks an oven. Trueblood staggered to the mess hall, listening to the complaints of the men around him without really hearing them.

He had no morning duty, being on sentry that week, and so, as the soldiers filtered out of the post, going about their various details, Trueblood walked to Pop Evans's and sat on the bench in front of the store. There was a mounted drill going on, Second Platoon participating, Corporal Miller overseeing it. It was nothing but a confusion of horses and dust to Trueblood.

He didn't know when Lieutenant Dunwoodie sat down beside him. Glancing at him, he saw the officer's tired eyes, his pale face. Neither man spoke. It might have been an hour, or even two, before Trueblood looked over again and noticed that Dunwoodie was gone.

One more night. That was all he thought of. One more night of watch duty. If he didn't get killed tonight, if he didn't get court-martialed for falling asleep, it would be over for a long while. He would work all day, sleep eight hours, and rise refreshed. Maybe it would cool off. Maybe this endless, damnable summer would end, maybe the sky would have mercy.

But there was no mercy. Trueblood moved like a zombie. Twilight was settling once again and he knew that this was the night. He knew that he would be shot and killed, and he didn't even care. It would be a blessing.

To die suddenly, to sleep forever. He trudged to the gate, his eyes only slits, his movements wooden and uncoordinated.

He went out immediately. He was two minutes early, but it didn't matter. It only meant he would die sooner. He followed the path, and rounding the first corner he felt like shouting out to the mad sniper: "Kill me, I'm as crazy as you are. Do me a favor."

Nothing happened. The post was quieting, settling in for

evening, when Trueblood got back to his post at the gate. Nothing had happened. He would survive. Everyone knew the sniper only fired at twilight, and Trueblood's last twilight on guard was fading to silky night.

He leaned against the wall and suddenly felt the rising emotion, the release of tears and laughter. Suddenly he was laughing and crying at once, and although there was no one around, Trueblood was speaking: "I'll be all right," he said, "it's only that it's been hot, I've been tired. And there's been the sniper. Christ, I'll be all right now."

"Going out?" Taylor asked, and Dunwoodie nodded.

The new lieutenant had a clean shave and had splashed some bay rum on his face—odd preparations for a man who was going out to stalk the sniper, Taylor thought.

Dunwoodie said nothing. He snatched up his gunbelt, which he had initially forgotten, and then, with a slight gesture of his right hand, he was gone. Frowning, Taylor followed him out. He stood and watched as Dunwoodie went to the tack shed to get his saddle, and then headed toward the paddock to emerge minutes later, mounted.

He trailed through the main gate and was gone. Taylor, shrugging, then glancing toward the captain's quarters, turned back toward the BOQ.

Trueblood saw Dunwoodie approach, snapped a salute, and was ignored. He watched the officer ride out onto the prairie and he wondered...

"I'm going out."

Trueblood turned to see Bill Fox standing in the shadows, a bunch of tools in his arms.

"What the hell are you talking about, Bill?"

"I want to go out, Trueblood. I've got a job to do."

"You're not supposed to go out."

128

"What's the difference? I'm not going over the hill, just turn your back for a minute."

Trueblood hesitated a moment and then turned away. What the hell did he care, anyway? Fox was going crazy, everyone knew it. Let him do what he wanted. One last night... Trueblood took a deep breath and looked to the milky stars. One more shift, one last night, and then let someone else have the worries.

On the hour, Trueblood went out to make his perimeter check. It was dark, warm, and silent. He was grateful for the last.

Nothing moved on the plains. Far off he could see firelight from the Indian settlement, and as he rounded the third corner, he heard briefly the sound of someone digging. The sniper? He didn't think so, and he didn't feel like investigating.

He didn't have to. Minutes later Bill Fox, shirtless in the night, his torso streaked with dirt, passed him.

"Fox?"

The man didn't answer. He was carrying two buckets, whistling as he went. Trueblood returned to the gate. He resumed his watch position, yawned mightily, and turned at the sound of an approaching horse.

It was Dunwoodie. And where the hell had he been keeping himself? Trueblood watched as the officer rode to the paddock and reappeared a time later, staggering as if wounded. Or weary. He watched him for a time; wondering. Then, with another jaw-cracking yawn, he turned away.

"Not tonight, Lieutenant," he promised himself, "you won't catch me sleeping tonight."

Taylor looked up from his book. Dunwoodie entered the room as if his feet weighed fifty pounds each. He had a

129

glazed look in his eyes, an odd, lost smile on his lips.

"You all right, Max?"

"Huh?" He didn't turn to look at Taylor. "All right."

"Are you sick, man?"

"No. Not sick." He turned and smiled again, the damndest, dumbest shit-eating smile Taylor had ever seen. "Thanks for taking duty for me."

"Sure..." Taylor was watching Dunwoodie closely. He looked exhausted, beaten, whipped, dragged, and battered. And he looked as if he had enjoyed the beating.

Dunwoodie nodded in Taylor's general direction and staggered out the door.

Three times. Dunwoodie surveyed the empty post, the dark skies, and he yawned. Three times again. Three times taken for a jolting, frenzied ride by those churning hips. He had a brief moment of doubt—what was he going to do about this situation? He couldn't ride out every night, screw the Cheyenne woman, and ride back to the post. He couldn't leave her out there forever; it was bound to rain eventually. Dunwoodie smiled at that and his doubts evaporated as he thought again of the pulsing heat of the woman, the sway and thrust of her.

Yawning, he moved stupidly on his round, lost in sensual reverie. She could take a man and pound him to dust. She was a hammering, throbbing joy of a ride.

The doors were all locked. Pop Evans's place was bolted up tight. The barracks were silent. Once he thought he heard a sound outside the stockade, a sound as if someone were digging, but he didn't have the ambition to go have a look just then.

He stood near the wall, watching the stars, his weary body relaxed and limp. He had been through an ordeal, a battle he had lost not once but three times. His eyes were heavy, and he needed just a moment's rest. Bracing himself

130

against the wall, Max Dunwoodie let his eyes droop shut. Just for a moment. Only for a moment while he thought of that Indian woman.

"Sir?" A hand shook Dunwoodie's shoulder and he placed his own on it, smiling. Then, with a start, his eyes flickered open.

He was sitting against the wall, his knees drawn up, and he had been soundly, criminally sleeping.

He jumped to his feet. Trueblood, his face ravaged by weariness, was facing him. "I'm going off duty now, sir, I figured I'd better wake you."

"I was—damn, I can't believe it. Sleeping! Thanks Trueblood, really. If the captain had come along. Jesus, thanks, I mean it!"

"It's nothing, sir," Trueblood said tiredly. "Nothing at all. It can happen to any of us."

Trueblood walked away then to meet Armstrong, who was coming on duty.

"Anything?" Armstrong wanted to know.

"Quiet as death," Trueblood replied. "Just as quiet as death."

ten

At daybreak, Lieutenant Matt Kincaid rode up the main street of Monument. Beside him rode Sergeant Gus Olsen and Private Aaron Shy. Behind him came a party of miners composed of Christopher Lacklander and his daughter Marie, Arnie Tabor, Clive Scales, George Bestwick, and a dozen other men who had gotten the word through one or the other of these.

"What is this?" Someone shouted from a window, and Tabor shouted back, "Kincaid's having a showdown with Toomey!"

Kincaid turned in the saddle, his mouth drawn into a frown. He was *not* planning on a showdown with the gunman, but that rumor had spread among the miners. He let the rumor flow unchecked, for his own reasons. He wanted

133

to get into and out of the Diamond Glen Saloon alive, and having a body of men with him was the easiest way to ensure that.

Aaron Shy had heard the rumor, and he now looked nervously at his officer. Shy didn't want to find out if he was a natural gunhand or not. The sinking feeling in his stomach caused him to believe that probably he was not.

"It's a showdown, all right," Kincaid said to Shy. "But not the kind everyone's hoping to see. I don't intend to shoot it out with anyone, nor to have anyone else fight."

Shy was puzzled, but he kept silent. Kincaid had some idea working in his mind, that was obvious. What it was, Shy couldn't guess. Behind them, people streamed out into the street, following in their tracks, wanting to see the gunfight. *How they love to see the blood flow—as long as it's someone else's,* Gus Olsen thought cynically.

Lifting his head now, he could see Frank Toomey on the porch of the Diamond Glen, watching their approach through narrowed eyes. He had his gang of thugs with him. Murray Hill, red-eyed and pasty-faced, unused to rising before noon, looked both menacing and competent. He had the flap of his coat pulled back behind his holster for easy access to the Colt that rode on his hip.

Toomey was sneering, but as Matt drew up and swung down from his horse, the sneer faded and Toomey's face grew stony, expressionless. His eyes, however, were alive, gleaming, vicious, quite deadly.

"What the hell do you want, Kincaid? I thought I told you to get out of Monument."

"It doesn't work that way," Kincaid said, keeping his voice under control.

"It does if Frank says so," Murray Hill put in. Matt ignored the gunhand.

134

"Shoot him!" someone in the crowd yelled, and it wasn't clear whether the speaker meant Toomey or Kincaid. Probably he meant both—anything for some harmless excitement. Shy looked over his shoulder nervously.

"Well, what is this?" Toomey asked, jutting his chin toward the mob. "A vigilante party? Come to chase me out of town, Kincaid?"

"No. I hope this will be a friendly visit, Toomey. It hasn't got a thing to do with you or your activities. I merely want to see the coffin in your back room."

"Hell, why worry about that?" someone shouted. "We'll make you a new one!"

"Go to hell," Toomey said almost automatically. He was considering, however. What kind of trick was this? Once Kincaid got inside, what would happen, would they smash up the tables and gaming wheels, destroy the liquor kegs?

"Let him in," Tabor said.

"Can't hurt you none," someone agreed.

"Go to hell," Toomey repeated unimaginatively.

"I'll see it one way or another," Kincaid told him. Now he stepped up onto the boardwalk, and Toomey seemed to flinch just slightly. Murray Hill took a step forward, his face set.

"What's the idea, Kincaid?" Toomey asked. Matt noticed from the corner of his eye that Olsen had positioned himself to one side of the gunmen. Gus was ready, but Kincaid wanted no shooting.

"I think there's something to be learned here," Matt said, trying to be reasonable. "I'd just like to see it. Everyone else in town has."

"It's a trick, Frank," Murray Hill said.

"Let him in!" a miner yelled. "Let's see what the lieutenant's got in mind."

Toomey vacillated; eyeing the huge, surging mob behind Kincaid, then glancing at his own men, he finally nodded agreement.

"All right," he said reluctantly. The crowd moved forward and Toomey angrily held up his hands. "Wait! I got something to say to you all. You can come through, but the first man who goes for the liquor is going to get shot through the guts. Hear me, Murray?"

Murray Hill nodded, then smiled dimly; things were looking up.

"I don't know what you're up to, Kincaid," Toomey snarled, "but have your damned look, then get out of my place and stay out."

Kincaid didn't answer. He strode in through the batwing doors of the saloon, the stale smells of last nights cigars and liquor filling his nostrils. A one-armed man was sweeping up, and he blinked in amazement as Kincaid, followed by fifty miners, tramped across his floor toward the back room where the coffin was kept on display.

Toomey led the way into the small room, and opened a window to let light and air in. Kincaid waited until everyone had settled down, and then he began his inspection.

"This is it, is it?" he asked. "Let me get this straight. This coffin was found up at the Danby Fork after the spring washout?"

"That's right."

"And inside?"

"There was a pile of bones," Scales said, "and of course the poke of gold."

"I see." Kincaid noticed the construction of the coffin, the lid of which was made with wagon-boards. "What happened to the gold?"

"Them that found it claimed it," a miner with a gray-streaked black beard answered.

"And you saw it?" Kincaid asked, turning to him.

"No." The man scratched his arm nervously. "Not me, I wan't around then. Maybe Clive or one of them."

"Clive Scales never saw the gold. Did you, Clive?" Kincaid demanded.

Scales muttered a negative.

Matt ran his hand along the coffin lid, his eyes narrowing. He had seen something, Olsen could tell that much. Kincaid knew something now, but what?

"Who was this man?" Matt asked the room in general. "What happened to him? When did he die?"

"I didn't kill him, if that's what you're thinking," Frank Toomey said with a smirk, and that brought a few laughs.

"We don't know for sure," Arnie Tabor said, becoming the spokesman. "We just know this man was found with a poke of gold dust in the coffin. Way we figure it, the man died—maybe Indians got him—and his partner must've hightailed it out, leaving the gold with the body for safekeeping. Poor bastard never made it back."

"No." Kincaid let his hand rest on the coffin. "When did this all happen, Arnie? I've heard it was a long while back, that it had to be a long while back, because if the strike had been recent, someone would have heard about it."

"Oh, yeah. It had to be a long while back," Tabor agreed. "Before there was any white men around here."

"It wasn't," Matt Kincaid said flatly. They looked at him as if he were crazy. But there was nothing except conviction on the officer's face. Olsen's eyes narrowed.

"You're crazy," Toomey put in.

"That coffin is old, maybe thirty years," Clives Scales put in. "Otherwise it don't make any sense."

"Because if it isn't that old, then word of the strike would have circulated."

"That's right. So you see, you're wrong, Kincaid."

137

"No," Matt shook his head definitely. "You are wrong, Scales. You, Tabor. You, Bestwick. You're all wrong."

"Go on!" someone said derisively.

"Listen," Matt said, facing each man in turn. "This is all a hell of a fine story, but there are a few points no one seems to have taken into consideration."

"Like what?"

"I'm getting to that right now," Kincaid said patiently. "First of all, no one I've run across has ever seen the poke of gold."

"Hell, no. They took it and run."

"Possibly," Matt agreed. "Secondly, unless I'm sadly mistaken, no one—*no one*—has ever found any gold in this area."

That brought a murmur of denial. They all looked anxiously at each other.

"Everyone that's got it is staying quiet about it," Tabor said.

"Possibly," Matt agreed again.

"Is that it, Kincaid?" Bestwick asked. "Is that your argument?"

"Not quite. Point three—this coffin isn't more than a few years old."

"The hell you say! It has to be older than that!"

"It doesn't have to be," Matt said, raising his voice above the clamor, "because it isn't. It just plain isn't, men."

"You're talking through your hat, Kincaid," Scales said angrily.

"No. I'm sorry, but I'm not. You boys are following a dream, and I hate to be the one to destroy a man's dreams, but I have to."

He turned back to the coffin, and pointed to one of its corners. "Did anyone take a good look at the *nails* in this coffin?" he asked the gathering.

All muttering stopped as several men in the crowd moved forward to examine the spot where the sides of·the rough-hewn box had been nailed together. There were loud gasps of astonishment, and one man who was wearing a carpenter's apron turned to face Kincaid.

"Well, I will just be damned," he said. "They're round-heads. *Wire* nails."

"Right," Kincaid said. "If this coffin were more than a few years old, it would have been put together with cut nails. Squareheads."

"Sure enough," the carpenter replied. "Hell, I still can't get roundhead nails 'cept now and then." He turned to address the assembled miners. "Boys," he said, "this here coffin can't be more'n two, three years old."

The miners were stunned into immobile silence. "I'm sorry, boys," Kincaid said, "but the coffin's new. Since it was put together such a short time ago, if there'd been a strike on the Danby, given the number of prospectors around here for the last five years, the news would have gotten around fast.

"Take that, couple it up with the fact that no one ever actually *saw* the poke of gold, add to that what you all know secretly about how much color you've found along the Danby, and I think you'll come to the same conclusion I have. I'm afraid there's not a nickle's worth of dust up there, or if there is, it sure as hell hasn't been discovered yet."

The silence was overwhelming. From time to time a man would push through the gathered crowd to take a look at the nailheads, but the others didn't have to look. They turned and walked slowly out of the saloon, faces blank, shoulders hunched, dreams shattered.

Finally there were only Lacklander and Marie, Toomey and his gunmen, and the three soldiers. "Well damn me for a Yankee," Lacklander kept repeating. "Damn me to hell."

Toomey was silent, but his eyes were speaking volumes. He was mad as hell. He could see the writing on the wall already.

"Get out, Kincaid," the saloonkeeper said savagely. "You've done enough, now get out."

"Now," Matt said, "I will, and gladly." Marie took his arm and went with him. Lacklander, after a last look at the coffin, shook his head and walked disconsolately after them.

Outside, the street was oddly empty, the town unusually silent. "So they had nothing?" Lacklander said finally. He was staring into space, looking toward the hills beyond the town. "Not Tabor, not Scales. None of them."

"No, sir," Matt told him. "That was what first bothered me. No one was shipping any gold out of here. And when I suggested that we figure out a way to do it, the response was far from overwhelming. Secretive a man might be, but he's got to find a way to bank his money unless he's a fool. No one was interested because no one had any gold."

They stepped into the street and walked toward the hotel, Marie still clinging to Matt's arm. In front of the hotel, Lacklander speculated, "Maybe Toomey himself started the rumors."

"Maybe, but it seems more likely he was sucked in like everyone else. After all, it wasn't the gold in the streams that drew him, but the gold in men's pockets."

"I suppose. I guess I was looking for someone to blame— someone besides myself, that is," Lacklander said with a weak smile.

"What'll you do now?" Matt wanted to know.

"Go back to the Black Hills, I suppose. The gold there is *real*, anyway." Lacklander stuck out a stubby hand. "I guess I should thank you, Lieutenant. I can say I won't forget you, nor Monument." He looked up and down the sunbaked street; then, shaking his head, he started back toward his horse.

Marie hesitated a minute. She looked up at Matt Kincaid, went to her tiptoes, and kissed him lightly and quickly on the lips.

"I won't forget you either, Lieutenant," she said, and then she too was gone, and Matt stood in the narrow ribbon of shade cast by the hotel awning, watching after her.

"Ain't love grand?" Olsen said, and Kincaid spun around. Then Matt grinned, slapped Olsen on the shoulder, and agreed.

"It's not bad, Olsen. Definitely not bad."

They had supper in a nearly empty restaurant and turned in early. Rising at dawn, Kincaid stood at the window, watching the street. Olsen stepped up beside him, drawn by the sounds of activity.

"Look at that," he said quietly. "Would you just look."

Private Shy joined them. The street was crowded with people. With wagons and buggies, with foot travelers and men on horseback. And they were leaving, streaming out of the town, leaving the houses, the shacks, the saloons deserted.

"Where in hell are they all going?" Shy wondered.

"Back to wherever they came from," Matt answered. "The dream's over. They woke up. And there's nothing left of it but the town. It won't be long before it's gone, as well. Monument, they called it. Well, I suppose it's a monument to something—to dreams, perhaps."

They dressed and shaved, packing their gear as the glittering sun peered in the window of the hotel room.

"You see, Private," Olsen told Shy, "when they send Matt Kincaid to do a job, he does it right. Cleaned this town right up, didn't he? No bloodshed, not much fuss. And you'll never see it done more prettily." Olsen scratched his

141

chin. "Of course, I ain't altogether sure it was what they had in mind."

The streets were deserted. It was an eerie walk to the restaurant. Here and there a bewildered storekeeper stood on the plankwalk, looking uptown and down. The restaurant was closed up tight. There was a hastily lettered sign in its window: *"Gone to Dakota."*

"What now, sir?" Shy asked. His stomach rumbled loudly enough for all of them to hear.

"Now? Let's get on home."

They walked to the stables and found the hostler perched on an empty keg.

"Still here, are you?" Kincaid asked.

"I'm gone as soon as you boys settle up," he said. He was acting nervously, and his eyes failed to meet Kincaid's.

"Something happen to the horses?" Matt asked.

"No," he said hurriedly. "No, they're fine. You owe me five dollars."

Matt paid him, wondering at the manner of the man. He didn't have to wonder for long. The hostler pocketed his money, grabbed his hat, and was gone, leaving the door open. Frank Toomey stepped in, sided by three of his men.

"Hello, Kincaid," he said softly, menacingly. Shy had hold of a saddle and now he dropped it, freeing his hands. "You've ruined me, you bastard," Toomey told him. "Emptied out my town. I told you I didn't want you nosing around."

"Back off, Toomey," Kincaid said. "It's not worth it. You lost some business, but there are other towns. You don't get a second chance at life."

"You ruined it all," Toomey said, and his voice was as soft and deadly as a rattler's buzz.

"There won't be many of us walk away from this," Matt went on, speaking softly. "Not at this range." He looked

142

at Hill and the other two hired guns. "You've nothing to gain, and a hell of a lot to lose."

"He's right, you know," one of the gunnies muttered. Toomey's head jerked around and he gave the man a look that could kill.

"You stay put, Weeks."

"*You* stay put," the gunman said. Then he turned and walked out the door. After a minute's hesitation a second man followed, with Toomey's curses chasing them into the harsh daylight.

"Bad odds, Toomey," Matt said now, and Toomey's eyes ran across the three competent-looking soldiers.

"You might be the one to get it," Toomey said, but his voice had a tremor in it now.

"Maybe." Matt shrugged indifferently. "But we're used to facing guns, to facing death. How about you, Frank, are you used to it?

Now Murray Hill spoke. "Let's get out, Frank."

Toomey's face was gray. He was damned scared, but he was determined. He spun on Hill. "You!" He laughed crazily. "I thought you were the gun hawk. The fast-draw man, the hero!"

"This just ain't smart, Frank," Hill replied. "Even if you kill him, we'll have the army on our butts from here on out. Chalk it up to experience. Me, I'm gittin'."

He turned away, and Toomey started shrieking. "You bastard! You cowardly bastard! You take my money and then you backwater on me. You'll shoot a drunk prospector in the back, but you haven't got the guts to—"

Frank Toomey's face twitched. He had lost control and Kincaid knew it. The saloonkeeper wouldn't listen anymore. He turned back, and Matt saw the gun come up in his hand.

Toomey's face brightened briefly with malevolent glee. His gun was out and coming up and Kincaid was just watching, watching coolly. Toomey would blast that coolness from his eyes. Damn the bastard!

Toomey had the hammer back, and his finger was squeezing down on the cool, curved trigger of the Colt when the mule kicked him. The mule kicked him square in the chest and then kicked him again. There was no pain, but he was slammed back against the stable wall.

A flood of heat washed over Toomey, and then with astonishment he saw that Kincaid had his gun in his hand, saw that smoke was curling from the muzzle, and too late Toomey understood what had happened.

Blood soaked his shirt front. That beautiful French silk shirt, and he looked at it uncomprehendingly. He felt the Colt in his hand, heavy as an anvil. It was hooked on his trigger finger still, but he could not lift it. And Kincaid— he had vanished behind a screen of blue and deep red-violet. Toomey watched as the pistol dropped free and fell to the floor of the stable. It seemed to take hours to reach the floor.

He started to say something, and found that his mouth would not work. "Damn you . . ." he managed before the blood, percolating up from his lungs, strangled off the rest of whatever it was he had to say.

He toppled forward and fell dead against the straw and manure-littered floor of the hostler's barn. Kincaid holstered his gun. Aaron Shy stood motionless, staring.

"Let's get on home, men," Kincaid said. "I don't think there's any more to be done here."

The streets of Monument were deserted as they trailed out, up the dry, dusty street. The sun beat down and the Belle Fourche, in the distance, glittered with sun-made jewels. Matt Kincaid never turned to look back.

eleven ━━━━━━━━━━━━━━━

"Sir?" Sergeant Cohen was at the door to his commanding officer's office, and Captain Conway looked up to see his first sergeant smiling. "There's a drifter out here who'd like to see you, sir."

"A drifter?" Before the puzzlement had washed out of the captain's face, Matt Kincaid appeared beside Cohen, and Conway rose smiling.

"Matt! Christ, come in."

"Sir!" Matt flashed a salute and Conway signaled to him to take a chair. Kincaid did so, and the captain took a bottle of bourbon from his bottom desk drawer and poured them both a glass. Then he perched on the corner of his desk, facing Kincaid, who was trail-dusty and sunburned.

"I kept hoping to God I wouldn't receive a wire from

you, Matt. I hoped it was something you'd be able to straighten out." Conway took a sip of his whiskey. "So, let's have the report. How did it go?"

Matt began to tell slowly about the Monument episode and Conway listened, trying to imagine how it had been. When Kincaid was through, he could only shake his head.

"A neat bit of detective work, Matt. Odd, wasn't it? All those men believing a myth. Well, I'm happy it worked out as well as it did. You'll have to have Olsen and Shy write up their versions of how Frank Toomey was shot, for your own protection, though I doubt anyone cares if the man died."

"I suppose not," Matt said. But it gave him no pleasure to think about Toomey slumped on the floor of the stable, his mouth filled with blood, hands twitching, sightless eyes staring. "How's everything on the home front?" Matt asked, to change the subject, "Quiet, I hope."

"Not exactly. Fitzgerald's still out on patrol. And we've got a little problem of our own right here." Conway outlined the problem briefly, describing the twilight sniper's activities. "I'd like to get Taylor and Dunwoodie in here and go over this more thoroughly, Matt. Thresh it out, see if we can't come up with some sort of solution."

Matt nodded. Something was ringing a small bell in the back of his mind, something he couldn't put a finger on or a name to. He didn't know why he believed it, but he told Conway, "I don't think it's an Indian, sir."

Conway looked startled. He leaned forward and told Kincaid, "Neither do I, Matt. Don't ask me why, but I don't either. It could be that imagination is running away with me, but I don't think it is some renegade. The main thing, of course, is to do away with all speculation, to find the sniper, whoever he is, and put an end to this before someone's killed."

146

Later in the afternoon, with Taylor and Dunwoodie present, they got down to brass tacks. Conway again ran over what had been done, searching the area, interviewing the local Indian population, and then asked what *should* be done. "Short of pulling out of Number Nine," he said with a shallow smile.

Kincaid knew the captain was worried. They had been together a long while, and he could read that expression. Taylor looked attentive but had no new suggestions, apparently. Dunwoodie looked distracted and tired. No doubt worrying about his fiancée, Kincaid thought.

He pointed out the obvious to the others. "The shots have been fired at twilight," Matt said. "Presumably the sniper then makes his escape under cover of darkness. The scout—Malone, right?—hasn't stumbled across the man."

"Nor any sign of him," Taylor put in.

"Just a minute, please," Kincaid said. "Let me get this out. The sniper fires at twilight and makes his getaway in the darkness. At neither time is it possible to apprehend him. Excuse me if I'm stating the obvious, sir," Matt said to Conway, "but when is the man getting *into* position? It has to be in daylight."

An obvious point, but one that no one had given much attention to. Conway mulled it over now.

"The time, then, to trap the sniper is while there is still daylight," Conway said.

Matt nodded agreement.

"I would think so. I believe, sir, we should post daytime sentries around the perimeter, and order them to watch all approaches to the post. If we're not dealing with a phantom here, he will have to make himself visible at one time or another."

"It'll disrupt routine," Conway said, but it was merely a grumbled complaint, not an objection to the plan, which was rational. "I'll have Ben set it up."

There being no further suggestions, Conway dismissed them. He managed to catch Dunwoodie before he left, however, and regretfully he told the junior officer, "I know you're anxious to get on to the Cheyenne garrison, Max, but I'm afraid I'm going to have to ask you to wait until I'm at full strength here with the present situation. Fitzgerald should be in within the week. At least I hope so."

"All right." Dunwoodie didn't seem disconcerted in the least. "No problem, sir. There's really no hurry. No hurry at all."

Conway was left to his puzzlement. Had Dunwoodie and that girl of his fallen out? He made a mental note to ask Taylor. Conway stood near the doorway a moment longer, then he called out for Sergeant Cohen and returned to his desk.

"What's this?" Rafferty asked no one in particular.

"Sentry roster," Wojensky told him. "Temporary perimeter sentry duty."

"The sniper," Rafferty said, understanding.

"That's it, pal. And lucky you, you made the list."

Rafferty had already found his name. He looked to the skies and turned toward the barracks. Holzer was already getting his gear together. Another fortunate soldier.

"You draw that sentry detail, Wolfie?"

"Ja!" Holzer responded, as if it were money from home.

Fox was giggling. "I got it too, Rafferty. Me and Brandt."

"Anyone sane going along on this?" Rafferty asked bitterly. "Or is this the way they chose us—all the nuts in one basket."

Fox chuckled away, Holzer was whistling. Brandt, in the corner, grinned dully, his dark eyes on Fox as he remembered his water-trough victory. Rafferty, perspiring in the ovenlike heat of the barracks, snatched up his canteen and his Springfield and walked out into the glare of the day.

"Tough luck, sport," Malone said.

"Yeah. Ain't it great?" Rafferty appealed once more to the heavens, got no response, and tramped over to the paddock, leaving a grinning Malone leaning against the porch upright.

Corporal Wojensky was in charge of this special watch, and he explained it to his first shift.

"This will work the same as guard duty—three hours on, three off, but we'll overlap the regular watch. The idea here is to spot anyone moving up near enough to the post to snipe at the guards. I should point out that he might also take a notion to fire a shot at you men."

A general groan went up at that point. Wojensky, holding up a hand for silence, went on.

"I won't tolerate any screwing off out there. The captain won't tolerate it. I can spot a man sleeping in the saddle for a long way. Remember, the life of one of your friends may depend on you keeping your eyes open. It could be your own life we're talking about."

Wojensky looked them over again, wondering at this first shift's makeup. Fox and Brandt together—didn't Cohen know about the friction there? Holzer would be okay, they didn't come any more reliable, and Rafferty was a good soldier. Wojensky looked at his watch.

"Let's go on out."

Rafferty had the south quadrant, and he rode out five hundred yards, feeling the dry wind in his face, the reluctant horse beneath him.

He drew up and shifted to look at the other two guards with him, Holzer and Fox. Brandt he could not see, because that man was riding the north quadrant, and the outpost stood between them. Drawing a deep, dry breath, Rafferty began to walk his horse back and forth, his eyes burning as he peered into the fierce light of the day. Wouldn't it ever cool off!

He walked his horse, seeing nothing but bare earth and occasional clumps of brush. He tried to stay alert, but it was impossible. The sun beat down, the detail was tedious, and despite the occasional shot of adrenaline his nerves gave him as a clump of brush moved in the wind, it was boring. Boring beyond words.

He saw nothing. He tried counting buffalo chips, tried remembering what that girl in Kansas City had looked like, how she had whimpered when he crawled on top of her— it didn't work worth a damn. He felt himself starting to go to sleep, remembered Wojensky's warning, and shook himself awake.

He stepped down, hoping the change of position would do some good, and drank from his canteen. Nothing. Nothing moved on the prairie. He could see Holzer riding in a zigzag pattern, see Fox standing in his stirrups. He could imagine Fox's giggling. With a sigh, Rafferty hung his canteen on the saddle and mounted, glancing at the sun, which told him he had not been out more than an hour.

From the corner of his eye he saw a frantic motion, and Rafferty spun his horse on its heels. Bill Fox was gesturing madly, though not in Rafferty's direction. He had given no shout, nor fired a warning shot.

Rafferty, who had given his horse a raking with his boot heels, now drew up in perplexity. Fox, still waving frantically, was not shouting an alarm, was not looking in his direction. He had his attention turned toward the northern quadrant where Amos Brandt was posted, and now Rafferty saw Brandt riding hell-for-leather toward Fox, who was yelling and waving him on. Rafferty kneed his horse into a canter and headed that way.

It was a puzzling alarm. No shots, no shout, just Fox waving his arm like a windmill in a gale, and Brandt riding wildly toward him. The sniper? Rafferty couldn't guess.

Then, in a moment, he didn't have to guess. Amos Brandt was riding at a dead run, Fox still waving him on, directing him, and then suddenly Brandt was gone, horse and all, and Rafferty saw a huge fan of muddy water splash up against the sky. Now he was near enough to see what had happened. Fox was doubled up with laughter, cackling hysterically, and Brandt, cussing the world and all of creation and most especially Bill Fox, was trying to drag himself up out of a muddy, six-foot-deep pit.

His horse was wild-eyed, only its head protruding from the pit, which had been filled with water and then covered with brush.

Fox must have dug it secretly, but when? At night apparently, filling it with water carried from the post. Then he had directed Brandt into it on the pretext of having found something.

Fox was laughing so hard he nearly tumbled from his horse. Brandt, coated with mud, was frantically trying to ride his horse up out of the pit, swearing a hundred oaths, all of which promised the destruction of Bill Fox.

"Think I'd forget that trough, Amos!" Fox shouted. "Think I'd forget who started this!"

Then he broke out in a fresh fit of laughing. And all the time Brandt was cussing, whipping his horse, his face a muddy mask.

Rafferty looked up to see Wojensky coming on the double, and he knew that this game was over for the time being.

"What in Christ's name is this!" Wojensky demanded of Rafferty, who only shrugged. "Help me get him out," Wojensky said wearily, and they tied on to Brandt's horse, dragging it up and out until the frantic bay had enough purchase to scramble away, bucking and twisting, spattering muddy water everywhere.

Fox had by this time actually fallen off his horse, and he sat there helpless with laughter, pointing a finger at Brandt, who had been thrown. Now Brandt, on hands and knees, tried to get at Fox, and Wojensky had to ride his horse between them. Wojensky wasn't a man quick to temper, but he had had enough. It wasn't the time or the place for this.

"You're both on report," Wojensky told them, and Rafferty knew he meant it. "Now get your butts back to the post and prepare yourself for a little conversation with Sergeant Cohen." To Rafferty the corporal said, "I'll send two replacements out. You and Holzer do your best till then." Then, as menacing as Rafferty had ever seen the man, Wojensky turned again to the two feuding men.

"God save your asses if someone gets picked off because of this horseplay, Fox, Brandt. I'll be coming after both of you myself. I promise you!"

Fox was no longer giggling. Brandt stood there, dripping muddy water, his face blank. Rafferty was glad he wasn't going to be there to see it when they got marched into Ben Cohen's office.

It was half an hour before Corporal McBride and Private Corson rode out and, after a minute's briefing, took up the positions vacated by Fox and Brandt.

"Watch out for a damned hole in the ground over there," Rafferty told Reb.

"Yeah, okay. I heard about it. I've got an idea Fox will

be out here filling it in tonight—with a teaspoon, probably."

Rafferty saw nothing the rest of his shift. They were relieved an hour later and rode in to supper. Malone and a very nervous-looking Stretch Dobbs were at a corner table, and Rafferty and McBride headed that way, trailed by Holzer.

"What fun, huh, boys?" Malone said. He was smiling, but his humor was growing a little dark as the days progressed. He produced a cold half-cigar from his shirt pocket and poked it in his mouth. Dobbs hadn't eaten. He was a little green around the edges.

"What's the matter, Stretch?"

"He's got the gate at twilight," Malone reminded them.

"Stay low," Rafferty said. His words didn't come out as lightly as he intended them to, either. "Hear about Fox and Brandt?" he asked, changing the subject.

"Hear about 'em!" Malone grinned hugely, touching a match to his cigar. "My God, boys, you could hear Cohen all the way across the parade. Damn fools."

"What time is it?" Stretch asked. His voice was a dry croak. He cleared his throat and tried again, flushing.

"Hell, Dobbsie," Malone told him, "don't be embarrassed in front of friends. You got a right to be scared. I would be."

"Five-thirty," Rafferty said.

"Who's with you?" Reb asked.

"Buckles, but I got the twilight," Stretch answered.

"He's probably long gone," Rafferty said. "Hell, the way we've been tramping around out there, I don't see how anybody could come up on the post."

"I wouldn't think so," Malone agreed. Somehow they didn't believe what they were saying. Somehow the twilight sniper had achieved mythic proportions, bigger than life, quieter than death, invisible as the wind. Maybe it was because no one had ever seen the man. Dobbs rose stiffly, nodded, and headed for the door. Malone's eyes followed him.

"Poor bastard," he muttered.

At twilight Malone, Rafferty, McBride, and Wojensky sat at a barracks table playing a desultory game of poker. No one was paying any attention to the cards, and twice the winner had neglected to rake in the pot. At dusk it was still enough to hear a pin drop. Holzer had glued himself to the window, watching as Stretch Dobbs made his rounds.

There was no betting on it—it had gotten too serious. Malone sat, holding one discard in the air, watching Holzer until finally the German turned and gave them the thumbs-up, a vast grin of relief on his face. Malone grunted and tossed the card down.

Someone sighed audibly. Turning, Malone saw Bill Fox sag back onto his bunk. He was as pale as a sheet. Brandt didn't look any better.

"What did Cohen say to them?" McBride asked.

"Nothin' much," Malone answered, deadpan. "Just that if that sniper got into position while these two were hoo-rahin' each other, he was going to have 'em shot."

"Shot!"

"Well," Wojensky muttered, "and what would you want done with 'em if the clowns let you get it?"

McBride nodded and threw down two pairs. "Aces and fours," he said, collecting the nickles. Outside it was nearly dark.

Two more nights passed, nearly as tense as the first. Stretch was beginning to look the way Trueblood had when he came off duty, but the sniper was lying low.

"He can't get near enough with patrols out all day,"

Rafferty said, and there was general agreement to that. Until the third night.

The shot came at twilight, and Malone nearly knocked over the table getting to his feet. He was to the door in three steps, but he was already behind McBride and Wojensky, who were sprinting for the gate, rifles in hand.

They found him outside the wall, writhing in agony. The sniper hadn't missed this time. Stretch Dobbs was down, and he was hit.

"Jesus Christ! Oh, Jesus!" Stretch rolled around, thrashing wildly, and Malone went to him, holding him still, forcing him down by the shoulders.

"Where, Stretch! Where did he get you, dammit!"

"Oh, goddammit!" Stretch yelled in frustration. "The arm, left arm."

Rafferty, Holzer, and McBride formed a sort of cordon around Stretch. Rifles at the ready, they searched the purpling plains, but there was no target. Nothing.

"Who is it?" Captain Conway asked breathlessly as he ran up.

"Dobbs, sir."

"Hit?"

"Yes, sir."

"Bad?"

Malone had Dobbs's shirt off, and the captain had to wait for the answer to his last question. Dobbs's arm was soaked with blood, and Malone could see a flap of skin peeled back like bark off a tree. But it didn't look all that serious. The artery and bone had been missed.

"He'll be all right, sir. At least I think he will."

Conway nodded soberly. You never knew with gunshot wounds. There was always the chance of gangrene, and with no surgeon...

Malone was binding the wound with a neckerchief, and

now he looked around for help. "Rafferty, let's carry him home."

"Did you see anything, Stretch?" Captain Conway asked, bending over his wounded soldier.

"Nothing, sir. God, it hurts!"

"You didn't see him?"

"Nothing, sir. Nothing at all."

Conway turned away. Holzer and McBride were still searching the prairie with their eyes, but already it was so dark they couldn't see ten feet in front of them. Conway heard a small sound and wondered what it was until he noticed that McBride was grinding his teeth together in frustration.

Conway understood that frustration. Damn it, show them the enemy and let's go at it. But this . . . this was not war, it was madness.

Flora opened the door to her husband, her eyes wide with concern. "Dobbs," Conway snapped, "hit in the upper arm. Lost a lot of blood. No sign of the sniper."

"Oh, no. Shall I see what I can do?"

"Maggie Cohen's with him. Go if you want to."

Conway's eyes were fierce, and Flora watched as he stalked to the liquor cabinet, poured a huge slug of whiskey, and paced the room. Flora dressed, and without bothering to pin up her hair, she slipped out. Matt Kincaid was on his way in.

"Watch yourself, Matt," Flora warned him. "You're liable to get your head snapped off." She placed an affectionate hand briefly on his arm and then was gone.

"May I come in, sir?" Matt asked, poking his head through the door.

Conway waved a hand. His face was grim. He poured a drink for Kincaid without asking, handed it to him, and said, "I want the bastard, Matt. It's no game any longer. This is priority. I don't care if it takes half of our people. I want the son of a bitch. Now! Before he kills someone."

twelve _____

Rafferty unhappily watched his shadow stretch out before him as the sun dropped lower toward the Rockies. Twilight was a time he had previously liked—a time when work was over for the day and there was a chance to relax, have a beer at Pop's, play some cards. Now it signaled danger. The prickling along the back of Rafferty's neck increased. He swallowed dryly.

"Anything?" Lieutenant Kincaid had set up this picket line, and he strode down the line of men who were posted a hundred yards apart, ringing the outpost. Malone had cynically termed it "a shooting gallery."

"No, sir, nothing at all," Rafferty replied.

Kincaid grunted something and kept walking. Corson was next on the line, then Hollis, and from then on, the line wound around the outpost so that Rafferty could not see them. But they were there, all standing watch, all tied up by a single man.

Who was he anyway, what the hell did he want? Rafferty shifted his feet and thought about that as he had a hundred times before. There was no answer. He was just a man who came and shot at soldiers and went away.

But how in hell did he get near enough? There was no cover on the prairie. Nothing but scattered brush, nothing big enough to conceal a man. He was good, whoever he was, he was damned good. Thank God the picket line seemed to be keeping him away; he hadn't made a try for four nights. Still . . .

Rafferty glanced over his shoulder, watching the sun sink below the dark horizon, knowing it would be a matter of minutes. It was the time of day they all sweated out now. Up and down the picket line, nervous glances were exchanged. Please, let it be someone else, not me.

But the picket line had scared him off—or at least that was the general opinion. A man would have to be crazy to fire on a soldier when there were fifty others to pursue him. But then, this man had to be crazy, didn't he?

Rafferty's shadow lengthened, blurred, and merged with the darkness that crept across the land. The twilight prairie was deep purple. Clumps of brush stood black against the flat earth. Furrows of shadow sketched lines of movement where there was no movement. The rifle in Rafferty's hands was cold, and his palms were sweating.

Nothing! He sighed with relief. It was damned near dark. He relaxed his grip slightly and turned his head. And the shot racketed across the plains. There was a scream of pain. Rafferty glanced to his right and saw Corson go down, writhing in pain. He searched for a target, saw none, and in anger fired anyway.

His shot triggered off a salvo, and the prairie was filled with rolling thunder and clouds of black powder smoke. Kincaid was coming on the double. Rafferty was running, stumbling toward Corson, who was gripping his thigh with both hands, his face a mask of pain, his teeth showing white.

"What happened?"

"Corson, sir!" Rafferty shouted, and before Kincaid could reach them, he was cutting away Corson's trouser leg. He had to tear Corson's hands away from the wound in order to examine it. Corson lay back, sweat raining off his face, teeth clenched, hands digging at the earth beside him.

"How's it look?" Kincaid asked.

"It's all right," Rafferty said for Corson's sake. It looked damned nasty as a matter of fact, but again the sniper had gotten mostly meat. The artery had been missed, and if the bone wasn't broken, Corson might make it.

"What in hell was all the shooting?" Kincaid wanted to know. "Someone see him?"

"No one saw him, sir," Rafferty said, and Kincaid could read the frustration there. He didn't press it.

"Get him inside," Matt ordered, and Holzer and Hollis cautiously picked Corson up. It wasn't carefully enough, however; a cry of pain escaped his lips as they got him up. Kincaid turned away.

He stood, simply staring at the prairie. Nothing moved. The darkness attacked and there was nothing anyone could do about it. In frustration the men had fired back, trying to kill the darkness, but it couldn't be killed. Resolutely, Kincaid turned. Captain Conway was going to be furious.

He was.

He was nearly to the gate when Kincaid met the captain. He had passed the wounded man, and now Conway asked stiffly, "Who was it?"

"Corson, sir."

"And all that damned shooting?"

"Frustration, sir. Someone touched off and they all joined in. Not very disciplined, but I can understand it at this point."

Conway only nodded. His mouth was absolutely grim. He stood there, staring out at the plains, until it was fully dark. Then he said hoarsely to Kincaid, "Find him, Matt. I don't care what it takes. Find him."

Taylor was in the BOQ when Matt returned, his eyes flinty, his jaw set. Kincaid didn't say a word for long minutes. Taylor didn't have to ask what had happened. Dunwoodie, moving like the living dead, walked in, picked up a small sack of supplies, turned, and went out. Matt hardly noticed.

Finally, with the lights out, Taylor asked him, "Well, what are you going to do now?"

"Get him," Kincaid said, and his voice had a murderous edge to it. "Those are my orders. That's what I intend to do."

He began an hour before reveille. Shaking out Rafferty and Malone, Kincaid saddled up while they dressed. In the paddock he explained what he wanted to do.

"We've got to search a larger area than we have up until now. The man is withdrawing in the daytime, but he can't go far. We're going to begin at the gate, and spiral out until we find him. You'll notice I didn't say I hope we find him, I didn't say *if* or *maybe*. I said *until we find him*."

The point was made. Rafferty and Malone exchanged glances and stepped into leather. Malone's bay nipped at his leg and he slapped its head away.

They rode out into the predawn. The prairie was gray and dry. A pale gray light announced the approach of the sun, and within fifteen minutes the horizon burst into life, flashing orange and rose against the dull skies.

They rode slowly, working with infinite patience, circling, searching the land. Kincaid didn't speak, nor did the enlisted men. They simply searched, hoping. By noon they were a quarter of a mile out, and they began to wonder if they had missed him again.

"He don't leave any tracks," Malone muttered. "None."

"He's got to be on foot," Rafferty said. "Can't wipe out a horse's tracks out here."

Kincaid said nothing. They had dry ham sandwiches prepared by Dutch Rothausen, and they munched them, drinking from the canteens. Kincaid waited until the last bite had been swallowed, then he was back in the saddle. Malone and Rafferty swung up as well and they began again the slow, patient circling, their eyes fixed on the ground, their nerves tingling.

In early afternoon they found her.

Malone nearly came out of his saddle. He expected to meet only one person on those plains—the sniper. He drew his pistol and went low behind the shoulder of his horse in one motion.

Then, taking a cautious second look, he saw it was a Cheyenne squaw, sitting there on a pile of furs, a little lean-to made out of canvas behind her. She was eating beef out of a tin, and she blinked in surprise at Malone, who stepped down and walked to her, pistol still in hand.

Malone turned and whistled shrilly. Then, trusting nothing, he dug through her belongings, searching for a Sharps rifle.

He found nothing. Kincaid was coming on the run, and he swung down from his horse in a cloud of dust, Rafferty behind him.

"What in hell? What are you doing here, woman?"

"Dunwoodie?" she said with a smile.

"Dunwoodie!" Kincaid repeated in astonishment. Then he noticed the supplies the woman had, all goods that Pop Evans carried. It was damned unlikely that a Cheyenne could have come by them.

"Dunwoodie," she said again, and again she smiled. Malone barked a laugh.

"Damn me if that don't beat all."

Kincaid just shook his head. "All right. Forget this, Malone, Rafferty. I'll straighten it out."

They swung onto their horses' backs and the woman stood, the tin of beef still in her hand. "Dunwoodie!" she called after them as they turned and rode slowly away. "Dunwoodie!"

Malone was grinning, but his expression altered rapidly as Kincaid, shooting him a hard glance, reminded them silently what their task was.

There was a last, distant cry: "Dunwoodie!"

They walked their horses in an ever-widening spiral, but there was nothing at all to arouse suspicion or interest. The earth was trackless, as if nothing had passed for a century.

They were north of the outpost and a mile distant when they came upon them. Dark, primitive, massive—a big buffalo herd drifting south. Kincaid, drawing up, cursed silently.

"They'll wipe out any tracks for sure," Malone said. He ran his sleeve across his sweating forehead. Nearly dark and still hot. He watched the buffalo for a long while. There were many thousands of them, moving southward in their dumb way, following the summoning of an ancient urge.

"It's damned near useless, sir," Rafferty said. "Once the buff get into the area around the outpost, there'll be nothing left to see."

"I'm aware of that, Private," Kincaid said, using a tone

that was stiff and short. He pondered it and decided illogically, "We'll stay out until daybreak. There might be something . . . I can't just give it up, boys," he said, and now his voice was more familiar. "The bastard's out here. I can feel it, I can damn near smell him."

Kincaid could just make out Number Nine, squat and dark against the plains. The buffalo were milling, preparing to bed down for the night. Twilight settled in.

"Let's spread our beds here," Kincaid said. Malone looked up in surprise. No one had said anything about sleeping out. Kincaid wasn't fooling around this time. He stepped down, and as his boot touched the earth, the shot rang out.

Malone froze. Rafferty flinched. The shot had come from near the outpost, and there was no mistaking the flat report of a Sharps. The sniper.

They swung into their saddles quickly, and Kincaid led out. There were only moments of twilight left, but Matt wanted to get closer to where the shot had been fired from. They circled wide, wanting desperately to keep the sniper between themselves and the post, to hem him in. Rafferty wondered silently who had been hit, who might have been killed. Their horses walked through the darkness until Rafferty felt Kincaid's hand touch his shoulder.

He held up and they swung down, squatting silently against the dark earth. They could see nothing by starlight, nothing at all, but they were near to where the sniper had fired from. They had to be near. Near enough to hear him if he moved.

They saw nothing. A dozen yards away the world became a black blur, empty and lifeless. They squatted silently, staring and listening. The buffalo herd, perhaps stirred to restlessness by the rifle shot, was moving nearer. There was the constant, distant scraping of hooves and an occasional muffled blatting. Nothing else. Malone grimaced, looking northward, hoping to God those buff didn't decide to start running.

It was a cramped, uncomfortable night. They dared not move, dared not roll out their beds. They were between the sniper and the buffalo herd. They simply waited, holding the reins to their horses, listening to the snorting and scuffling of the buffalo herd, watching the night for some indication of the sniper's presence.

The night passed slowly—a dry, empty night, with the sound of the buffalo herd ever nearer, the herd itself invisible in the darkness. Malone's muscles knotted up, and tension and dry heat caused his pores to trickle perspiration. He must have been as uncomfortable at other times, but he couldn't recall when. They sat and waited, watching for the sudden movement of the sniper—or for the sudden rumbling charge of the buffalo.

Malone's horse took a good nip of his ear. It was simply the topper; he couldn't even get mad about it.

At first light they mounted and spread out, watching the barren prairie. Kincaid kept motioning them back, away from the outpost, not wanting to let the sniper break through, for Matt was sure he was still there, between them and the post. He had to be. *Had* to be. But a phantom doesn't *have* to be anything.

Now, with deep frustration, Matt Kincaid studied the buffalo herd, which seemed to have grown larger during the night. They were drifting southward, steadily southward, directly toward Outpost Number Nine, and they were between Kincaid and the post. There would be absolutely no sign of anything on the earth when the buffalo were through.

"The bastard's going to get away with it," he thought sourly. "He's going to get away with it again." The rising sun was in his eyes, casting long shadows before the low-growing clumps of sage. The buffalo advanced slowly, inexorably, and Kincaid was ready to throw up his hands in despair. They would overtrack anything useful, leaving nothing but thousands of buffalo tracks—a situation that even Windy Mandalian would find impossible.

He turned, halting his horse, watching the massive herd flow toward them. There was a danger of the herd turning, and he didn't want his men in their path if they did so. Might as well go in, he decided, as much as it rankled him. Might as well go in and admit the man was too much for them...

Matt had turned, lifting his hand to summon Malone and Rafferty, ready to give just that message, when something drew his vision. Some movement seen from the corner of his eye. Some incongruous motion. It seemed as if—but it couldn't have been—it seemed as if a clump of sage had slowly—almost imperceptibily—*moved*. Kincaid blinked and looked again, hardly trusting his eyes.

Malone and Rafferty, answering their officer's summons, reined in beside Kincaid.

"What—?" Malone began, but Kincaid motioned him to silence.

Matt's finger was leveled at a clump of brush nearly half a mile away. Malone, shading his eyes with his hand, stared that way. He saw nothing at first, and then—by God—a clump of brush moved! Definitely moved. Rafferty saw it now too.

Behind it the buffalo moved placidly forward, shearing grass and brush as they roamed southward. "Let's have a look at that," Kincaid said, his eyes narrowed, his lips compressed.

He stepped into the saddle and kicked his horse into motion. They rode directly toward it, still uncertain. It had ceased to move—if it had been moving at all. They were

167

within five hundred yards when it happened.

The clump of brush suddenly rose, a dark rectangle against the low sun, and Kincaid stood in his stirrups. He could see a man in silhouette. There was only one man he expected to find out on these plains, and he kneed his horse, urging it on as he shifted his Springfield.

The sniper—it had to be the sniper—had obviously seen them, and now he was up and running, sprinting toward the buffalo herd.

"He's trying to get to the other side of them!" Kincaid shouted above the drumming of the horses' hooves. And if he made it, he had a good chance of making his escape. Kincaid spurred his horse on, Malone and Rafferty beside and behind him, as they pursued the fleeing sniper across the empty plains.

They were gaining fast, Kincaid knew, and now the sniper himself seemed to realize he wasn't going to make it. He went down on one knee and fired three shots, all of them falling short. In desperation the man scrambled to his feet and began running again. But Kincaid was closing the gap rapidly.

They were within three hundred yards of the sniper, not much farther from the buffalo herd. Kincaid drew up sharply and shouldered his rifle. He was damned if the man was going to get away. He fired, saw the dust kick up at the sniper's foot, reloaded, and fired again as Malone's rifle echoed in his ear.

The sniper was nearly around the head of the slow-moving herd, and for a minute Kincaid felt frustration and savage anger. That herd, miles long, would screen the sniper off effectively.

Rafferty fired, and then Malone again. Kincaid squeezed off another shot and the sniper whirled, possibly tagged. He raised that carbine of his and fired. The bullet whipped past Kincaid's ear. Matt shoveled a fresh cartridge into the breech and fired again.

"Look out!" The voice was Malone's, and Kincaid glanced at him sharply, not understanding at first. And then he did. The buffalo herd seemed to lift itself into motion like a vast, single living creature. Their heads came up as one, and the thunder of their hooves was like cannon fire. The herd, startled by the close rifle fire, lifted into a run, and within moments it was a headlong stampede.

The sniper, on his knee for another shot, was directly in their path. By the time he realized his danger, it was already too late. He forgot about shooting, and took off at a mad veering run, but he failed to make it.

The herd, turned by the approaching Easy Company men, swung toward him and then he was gone. There was a flash of color, a shirt or a scarf maybe, and then he was sucked down into the brown, rolling sea, soundlessly dying, being trampled into the earth by the mammoth herd, which rolled on like an angry behemoth.

"Stop that damned herd!" Matt yelled, aware of the danger before the others. "Shoot the leaders."

Malone hesitated; it was too late by far to save the sniper. What was Kincaid thinking thinking of? Suddenly it dawned on him, and with cold determination he began trying to take down the leaders of the herd.

It was far too late to save the sniper, and now as the vast waves of bison thundered past, Malone feared what Kincaid knew was a possibility—it might damned well be too late to save Outpost Number Nine. The herd, awesome in size and weight, unstoppable as it rushed on in blind panic, had turned directly toward the outpost.

thirteen ━━━━━━━━━━━━━━

Reb McBride was on the picket line, still thinking of the near miss he had had last evening when the sniper had cut loose again. He was aware of it subconsciously before his brain measured and categorized the danger. A distant rumbling, a dark, vast movement, like an angry sea.

Peering into the morning sun, he heard it. Then there was a flurry of shots. McBride saw Kincaid and his soldiers riding hell-for-leather, and then it registered—sharply.

That buffalo herd was running—running blind—and had turned directly toward the outpost.

"Holzer! Hollis!" Reb shouted to the men nearest. Holzer's head came around and McBride, frantically pointing, got the message across. Hollis took one look at the thundering herd and took off at a dead run. McBride wasn't far behind.

The men from the picket line hit the front gate as the rumble of hooves became audible everywhere. Work stopped immediately. Heads lifted and faces wore puzzled expressions. Suddenly a shout went up. Warner Conway dashed from the orderly room, Sergeant Cohen at his shoulder.

"What is it?"

McBride, who had run a good quarter of a mile, panted his answer: "Buffalo herd, sir! They're heading dead at us."

Flora Conway and Maggie Cohen had appeared from somewhere. Trueblood and Armstrong were sprinting across the parade. Pop Evans stood before his store, his pinched face set in confusion.

"Get up on the roof," Conway ordered immediately, his command taking in every man in sight. "Take down the leaders of that herd, or, by God, we'll be left in charge of a pile of kindling."

Reb McBride was already on his way before Conway had finished speaking. He knew perhaps better than any of them what a buffalo stampede could mean. Years ago a herd had overrun the camp of a trail drive he was with. There hadn't been enough left of the men who were trapped in front of the herd to identify them as human beings.

Reb was on the roof now, and the buffalo seemed nearly on top of Number Nine, although they were still a good distance off. Clouds of dust spumed into the skies, and the thunder rocked the outpost beneath McBride.

He fired, saw a big bull buff go down, reloaded, and fired again. Trueblood was beside him and he fired too, and they fired until their rifle barrels were hot. They weren't alone. All along the parapet, Easy Company fired and fired again, and still the buffalo came on.

"We're not going to stop them! Nothing's going to stop them!" Trueblood shouted. He had visions of himself going down beneath the thousands upon thousands of razor-sharp hooves, sucked down into that woolly brown sea.

"Keep shooting," McBride snarled, but with a sinking heart he realized that Trueblood was probably right.

Above the rumble and thunder of the hooves, Reb heard someone shouting. It was Ben Cohen, whose voice was audible even above an artillery barrage.

"Lend a hand, goddammit! Open the gate!" Reb looked over the inside edge of the parapet, and saw Ben Cohen racing toward the gate, hauling behind him the Gatling gun on its large-wheeled limber. McBride scrambled down the ladder and raced for the gate, whose usual contingent of guards had gone up to the parapet to help fend off the stampede. He slid aside the massive timber bolt and swung the gate open just as Cohen arrived and swung the gun around so that its barrel faced out through the gate, pointing toward the advancing brown wave.

"Load me!" Cohen bellowed as he jammed chocks under the limber's wheels and climbed up onto the wagon. McBride, meanwhile, had opened the ammo chest, and now he leaped up onto the limber beside Cohen and shoved a magazine into the top of the weapon's breech. Cohen had finished attaching the gun's trigger-crank, and he began to turn it, sweeping the barrel back and forth along the width of the stampede's advance. Flame and powder smoke erupted from the Gatling's barrel, and buffalo began to go down all along the front ranks of the herd. When the gun clicked empty. McBride unclipped the spent magazine and affixed a fresh one, praying that the temperamental gun wouldn't jam, as was its annoying habit under these conditions.

And then it was done. The buffalo split to clear the fallen bodies of their leaders and the stampede parted, trailing past the outpost in a seemingly endless stream.

Cohen reached over and clapped McBride on the back. "Plenty of buff steaks, eh, Reb?"

"Plenty of steaks," Reb agreed weakly.

Cohen grunted and started away across the parade, calling back, "Come see me about that pass, McBride."

"So that's what it takes to get a pass out of him," McBride muttered, shaking his head.

Outside, the herd's dust had begun to clear somewhat, and it was with vast relief that through the thinning cloud McBride discerned three blueclad figures riding across the prairie.

Kincaid looked down at the ragged, crumpled figure pressed against the earth. The man should have been dead, but he wasn't. The sniper lay broken and trampled, but he was still living.

"Look here," Malone said, and Kincaid, glancing that way, saw the blind that the sniper had used to conceal himself. A light burlap-covered frame with grass and brush covering its top, it blended in so well with the prairie that it would be invisible from more than a few yards away.

The dust was heavy in the air, the sun hot, the horses sweating from the long run. The sniper had the look of death on him.

Kincaid swung down and moved nearer, sickened by the sight. The man's chest had been crushed. A broken arm dangled uselessly, and telltale blood frothed from his mouth. Enough of his ruined rifle lay close by for Kincaid to identify the deadly, accurate .45-90 Sharps.

Kincaid's shadow crossed the battered face of the sniper and his head came slowly around. Haunted eyes fixed on those of the officer. Anger still floated in those eyes, a terrible hatred, and it jolted Matt.

A hatred like that, a hatred lingering to death, is a terrible

174

thing, and to Kincaid it was inexplicable. He had to know.

"Why?" he asked, hunkering down next to the sniper. "Who are you? Why did you do it?"

The man's eyes slowly swept past Kincaid, focused on some distant point, and then returned, the sharp loathing still dancing in his eyes.

"Why..." His voice was a blood-choked burble. "I...the army took it all. Everything that meant anything..." He coughed violently, spitting up a pint of blood. It ran down his chin and coated his neck and chest.

"What do you mean!" Kincaid shouted at him. "I have to know, man!"

"Tell you..." He began wearily, closing his eyes tightly, his chest rising and falling spasmodically as the broken ribs inside did their damage with each breath. "Engels...that's my name. I'm a wolfer by profession." He coughed again and Kincaid had to look away. It was a long while before he could speak again. He lay staring at the sky, his eyes glassy now.

"Tell me, Engels!"

"Engels...wolfer. Had a cabin up on the North Platte..." his voice faded out, but he managed to bring it back. "Had a cabin...where my wife and my babies stayed while I worked my traplines. The army..." He spat the word out. "The army promised to keep an eye on the cabin while I was off. But the Cheyenne come one day...come and killed 'em. Killed my wife. Killed my kids. And the army didn't do a damned thing about it!"

"Engels!"

He had drifted into deep twilight, the twilight of pain and approaching death. He looked at Kincaid without seeming to see him.

"I'd a' killed you all, given time," he said faintly. "Killed you all..."

175

And then he said no more, he lay back, a broken image of a man, his hatred dying with him. Kincaid stood and stared at the body, wondering at it.

"Can you beat that?" Malone said.

"I guess in his mind he had reason," Rafferty added. "What post would that have been, Lieutenant?" the soldier asked. "There ain't any garrison up that way close, is there?"

"There was." Kincaid turned slowly, his eyes distant. "Fort Casper. It was closed down ten years back."

fourteen ─────────────

"Ten years," Warner Conway said in amazement. "And that hatred was building all the time, looking for a release he never found."

"Until he came here," Kincaid said.

Windy Mandalian sipped some of the captain's good whiskey and commented, "That's the way it is with a crazy man. It festers and the man grows sour. You never know when it's going to come out."

"And Engels was mad," Conway said.

"Stark looney," Windy said. "But clever. It seems to me a lot of crazy folks are foxy like that. Damn smart in a crooked way."

"I don't see how he got away with it, hiding out there," Dunwoodie put in. The captain offered the bottle around again. Fitzgerald, Taylor, and Dunwoodie declined. Kincaid took a splash and Windy, still dry from the trail, helped himself freely.

The old scout settled back in his chair. "Wolfers are a clever lot, son," Mandalian told him. "They can hide themselves so you have to trip over 'em before you'd find 'em. Like an Indian, they are. Have to be."

"Have you heard of anything like that blind he was using, Windy?"

"Oh, yeah. That's not a new trick, but from what you tell me, he was good at it. Might've puzzled me for a few days," Windy said.

"It took us a few weeks and a herd of buffalo," Kincaid had to admit.

"It's all in the experience, Matt," Mandalian said. "Me, I've wolfed a little and seen a few things. Anything like this comes up again, you'll know."

"I'll never forget," Kincaid said soberly.

"Ten years," Dunwoodie said, shaking his head in amazement.

"Hell of a long time to carry anger—or grief," Warner Conway said. "Well"—he rose from behind his desk— "maybe we can get things back on an even keel again. The sniper's gone, rest his soul. Fitz and Windy are back—and I imagine both of them would like to get some rest."

"Wouldn't mind it, sir," Fitzgerald said, rising.

"And I imagine Lieutenant Dunwoodie would like to be on his way to the Cheyenne garrison—with our thanks."

"Thank you, sir," Dunwoodie said, taking the captain's hand. "I learned a lot."

"So did we all." Warner Conway shook his head. "It seems we learn something every day out here, doesn't it?"

They rose and filed out, leaving Conway to his reports.

Fitzgerald and Taylor wheeled off toward the BOQ. Dunwoodie stood looking quite unhappy, his eyes vacant.

"Hold up, Dunwoodie," Matt Kincaid called. "Just a minute." He ducked into the orderly room and returned a minute later with Windy Mandalian. "I think this is the man who can help you."

"What do you mean?" Dunwoodie asked nervously.

"We found her out there," Matt said, and Dunwoodie swallowed hard. Windy looked from one man to the other, his eyes narrowed. "Best tell Windy all about it," Matt suggested.

Windy listed to Dunwoodie's tale of winning the squaw from Blue Hand, of not knowing what to do with her. "And now I've got to get to Cheyenne, Windy. What the hell can I do?"

"Give her to me," Windy said. His eyes were twinkling.

"What?"

"I'll take her off your hands. I'll trail down home and tell them that you give her to me. Of course," he said with a wink, "Quiet Eyes won't like that a bit. She'll make me get rid of her. I imagine sooner or later I can manage to lose her back to Blue Hand—he likes a horse race now and then."

Dunwoodie looked as if the weight of the world had been lifted from his shoulders. He took the scout's gnarled hand and pumped his arm vigorously. "Thanks, Windy. Thanks so much. I can't thank you enough."

"Don't give it another thought, young feller," Windy said. "Just do yourself a favor and don't gamble with a Cheyenne again."

"Never again," Dunwoodie agreed with a huge grin. Then he turned and walked off toward the BOQ, whistling as he went.

"I don't know how in hell we ever get along without you, Windy," Kincaid said, leaning against the rail. The scout just laughed.

"I don't either, Matthew. I swear I don't either!" Then Mandalian was gone, swinging a long leg up over the back of his appaloosa horse. Matt waved and turned back toward the orderly room.

Something caught his eye and he glanced skyward, noticing only now that the day had cooled. Vast fields of gray clouds were blocking out the sky, and as he watched, the first huge raindrops began to fall. The heat wave had broken.

Matt stepped toward the orderly room door and had his hand on the knob when he heard a gigantic splash, as if the skies had decided to drop the rain in barrels. Then, moments later, the sound of Bill Fox's crazy giggling echoed across the parade. Kincaid didn't even look back. He went on into the orderly room, closing the door firmly behind him.

Watch for

EASY COMPANY AND THE SHEEP RANCHERS

twenty-first novel in the exciting
EASY COMPANY series from Jove

Coming in October!

EASY COMPANY

RIDE THE HIGH PLAINS WITH
THE ROUGH-AND-TUMBLE
INFANTRYMEN OF OUTPOST NINE—
IN JOHN WESLEY HOWARD'S EASY COMPANY SERIES!

____	05761-4	EASY COMPANY AND THE SUICIDE BOYS #1	$1.95
____	05804-1	EASY COMPANY AND THE MEDICINE GUN #2	$1.95
____	05887-4	EASY COMPANY AND THE GREEN ARROWS #3	$1.95
____	05945-5	EASY COMPANY AND THE WHITE MAN'S PATH #4	$1.95
____	05946-3	EASY COMPANY AND THE LONGHORNS #5	$1.95
____	05947-1	EASY COMPANY AND THE BIG MEDICINE #6	$1.95
____	05948-X	EASY COMPANY IN THE BLACK HILLS #7	$1.95
____	05950-1	EASY COMPANY ON THE BITTER TRAIL #8	$1.95
____	05951-X	EASY COMPANY IN COLTER'S HELL #9	$1.95
____	06030-5	EASY COMPANY AND THE HEADLINE HUNTER #10	$1.95

Available at your local bookstore or return this form to:

J JOVE/BOOK MAILING SERVICE
P.O. Box 690, Rockville Center, N.Y. 11570

Please enclose 75¢ for postage and handling for one book, 25¢ each
add'l. book ($1.50 max.). No cash, CODs or stamps. Total amount
enclosed: $ _____ in check or money order.

NAME _____

ADDRESS _____

CITY _____ STATE/ZIP _____

Allow six weeks for delivery.   SK-4

EASY COMPANY

MORE ROUGH RIDING ACTION FROM JOHN WESLEY HOWARD

_____ 05952-8	EASY COMPANY AND THE ENGINEERS #11	$1.95
_____ 05953-6	EASY COMPANY AND THE BLOODY FLAG #12	$1.95
_____ 06215-4	EASY COMPANY AND THE OKLAHOMA TRAIL #13	$1.95
_____ 06031-3	EASY COMPANY AND THE CHEROKEE BEAUTY #14	$1.95
_____ 06032-1	EASY COMPANY AND THE BIG BLIZZARD #15	$1.95
_____ 06033-X	EASY COMPANY AND THE LONG MARCHERS #16	$1.95
_____ 05949-8	EASY COMPANY AND THE BOOTLEGGERS #17	$1.95
_____ 06350-9	EASY COMPANY AND THE CARDSHARPS #18	$1.95
_____ 06351-7	EASY COMPANY AND THE INDIAN DOCTOR #19	$2.25
_____ 06352-5	EASY COMPANY AND THE TWILIGHT SNIPER #20	$2.25

Available at your local bookstore or return this form to:

J JOVE/BOOK MAILING SERVICE
P.O. Box 690, Rockville Center, N.Y. 11570

Please enclose 75¢ for postage and handling for one book, 25¢ each
add'l. book ($1.50 max.). No cash, CODs or stamps. Total amount
enclosed: $ _____ in check or money order.

NAME _____

ADDRESS _____

CITY _____ STATE/ZIP _____

Allow six weeks for delivery.   SK-4